PRESENTED TO:

....

FROM:

....

— DATE:

....

BELIEVE IN YOU

Big Sister Stories

and Advice on Living Your Best Life

Christina, Katherine, Lisa, Amy,
Lauren, and Danielle Cimorelli

An Imprint of Thomas Nelson

© 2019 Christina, Katherine, Lisa, Amy, Lauren, and Danielle Cimorelli

Some of the material in this book was previously published as *Lessons Learned*.

Published in Nashville, Tennessee, by Tommy Nelson. Tommy Nelson is an imprint of Thomas Nelson. Thomas Nelson is a registered trademark of HarperCollins Christian Publishing, Inc.

Authors are represented by the literary agency of The Fedd Agency, Inc., P.O. Box 341973, Austin, Texas 78734.

Tommy Nelson titles may be purchased in bulk for educational, business, fund-raising, or sales promotional use. For information, please e-mail SpecialMarkets@ThomasNelson.com.

Unless otherwise noted, Scripture quotations are taken from the *New American Bible, revised edition.* © 2010, 1991, 1986, 1970 Confraternity of Christian Doctrine, Washington, DC. Used by permission of the copyright owner. All rights reserved. No part of the New American Bible may be reproduced in any form without permission in writing from the copyright owner.

ISBN 978-1-4002-1928-5 (Signed edition)

Library of Congress Cataloging-in-Publication Data

Names: Cimorelli, Christina, 1990- author.
Title: Believe in you : big sister stories and advice on living your best
life / Christina, Katherine, Lisa, Amy, Lauren, and Danielle Cimorelli.
Description: Nashville : Tommy Nelson, 2019. | Includes bibliographical
references.
Identifiers: LCCN 2019027067 (print) | LCCN 2019027068 (ebook) | ISBN
9781400213023 (hardcover) | ISBN 9781400213030 (epub)
Subjects: LCSH: Preteen girls--Conduct of life--Juvenile literature. |
Teenage girls--Conduct of life--Juvenile literature.
Classification: LCC BJ1651 .B398 2019 (print) | LCC BJ1651 (ebook) | DDC
248.8/33--dc23
LC record available at https://lccn.loc.gov/2019027067
LC ebook record available at https://lccn.loc.gov/2019027068

Printed in the United States of America

19 20 21 22 23 LSC 10 9 8 7 6 5 4 3 2 1

Mfr: LSC / Crawfordsville, Indiana / September 2019 / PO # 9549948

CONTENTS

INTRODUCTION

WHEN WE STARTED TOURING AND recording as Cimorelli, we had no idea we'd get to have the incredible privilege of meeting so many girls and hear their stories. For every song and video we've poured our hearts into and shared with the world, we've gotten just as much back from people who've poured their hearts out to us. All six of us sisters—Christina, Katherine, Lisa, Amy, Lauren, and Dani—have been touched by the thousands of messages on social media, hundreds of letters pouring into our PO box, and beautiful encounters at meet and greets where we started to hear personal stories from the girls we met everywhere we went.

And these weren't just inspiring, uplifting stories. They were the real stories of what girls were going through. Intense, heavy things. Stories of body image and self-esteem issues, eating disorders, depression and anxiety, toxic friendships, relationship problems, and broken families. So many personal details from the hardest parts of life as a girl—and things some of us have been through ourselves. All we wanted to do at that point was be there for these girls, to support them and be a group of big sisters to every single person who shared her story with us.

For the longest time we wore ourselves out, replying to as many requests for advice and help as we possibly could. But we got more and more frustrated as the messages and letters continued to pour in and we realized we could not reply to all of them. How could we possibly convey to you how much we believe in you? And how much *you* deserve to believe in you?

The answer? This book.

One afternoon we sat down and asked each other, "What do people ask us for advice on the most?" The answers gave us the idea for these chapters. We think they cover some of the most important things girls wonder about during teenage years: your relationship with yourself, spirituality, friendship, dating, family, money, and the uncertainty of the future. You're going to hear our real, raw, unedited take on each and every one of these topics.

As you read these chapters, picture us speaking right to you. We've truly poured out our hearts to give our most honest advice and share our stories and struggles without sugarcoating it, but to focus on the positive too. Because as hard as it can be, growing up is also one of the most important experiences we have as humans. It's not all just struggle and pain (even when it feels like that sometimes)—it's also fun and exciting as you get older and experience more freedom and self-discovery. There's so much to get excited for in the years ahead. We can tell you because we've gone through those years and come out the other side.

How could we possibly convey to you how much we believe in you?

All six of us have unique, very different personalities and experiences. Some of us are shy and introverted, others bubbly and outgoing, some fiery and driven, others peaceful and sensitive. We're guessing that every girl who reads this will relate to each

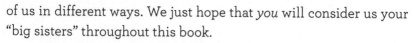

of us in different ways. We just hope that *you* will consider us your "big sisters" throughout this book.

Growing up can be difficult, confusing, awkward, and scary, but it's a lot better when you have someone to go to for advice and some words of encouragement. You need to hear that someone believes in you—and that you're *worth* believing in. We firmly believe that about you. So, take this book as a hug and some big-sister assurance that you are not alone in learning some of life's greatest lessons.

CHAPTER 1
YOUR RELATIONSHIP WITH YOU

ONE OF THE GREATEST CHALLENGES of becoming a teenager is learning to love and take care of ourselves—our bodies, hearts, and minds. Because let's face it: sometimes we feel like a mess, and it's hard to know what to do about it. We've been there, and we want to encourage you that even through your ups and downs, *you* are worth loving and investing in, getting to know, and taking care of.

We are going to talk a lot in this book about your relationships with others, including your friends, family, and boys, to name a few. But to start with, we want you to know that your relationship with yourself is priceless, because it affects everything about you!

In our family, we sisters have a ten-year age range between us—from nineteen to twenty-nine. The "older generation" among us had a hard time figuring ourselves out growing up because we didn't really have the role models to guide us through adolescence. We had to figure it out on our own, through trial and error and with limited help from some of the American Girl advice books.

Even though your ups and downs, you are worth loving and investing in, getting to know, and nourishing.

As teens, the millennials among us were given all sorts of different messages from articles in *Seventeen* magazine, reality TV shows, and so on. Then the Gen-Z sisters had to deal with messages from social media influencers, Snapchat articles, and Instagram. No matter where we see them, though, titles like "7 Tips to Have a Great Hookup" and "How to Get a Bikini Body" can be confusing and toxic when we're still asking ourselves, *Who am I, now that I am becoming a woman? A sexual object, like these titles say? Does being "beautiful" and looking "perfect" make me valuable?*

And on top of all those questions, there's the physical stuff. How do we take care of ourselves with all the hormones and changes in our bodies and emotions? It can feel overwhelming. But you don't have to go through it alone.

So first things first; let's talk about cultivating a healthy heart, mind, and body so you can approach every day with growing strength and confidence. You *can* have a good relationship with yourself. It just takes a little bit of perspective and some good habits.

> [Be] confident of this, that the one who began a good work
> in you will continue to complete it until the day of Christ
> Jesus.
>
> PHILIPPIANS 1:6

DEALING WITH THE NEGATIVE

There are so many messages out there trying to tell us who we should be and what we should want for ourselves. How do we figure out what standards are right for us and which ones are just over the top?

Lauren

It's really easy to put these impossible standards on yourself. For instance, "My makeup has to be perfect. My outfits have to be perfect. My hair has to be perfect. I have to be perfectly in shape. I need to get perfect grades, make fun and cool friends, and have perfect, fun, and exciting conversations with them *all the time*. I need to get a perfect boy, who thinks I'm perfect."

The list goes on. But when it comes down to it, the only person who can choose your standards is *you*—so give yourself a break. The truth is, if you try to measure yourself against the world's standards, you'll never measure up, because they're not humanly attainable. You'll spend your whole life never feeling good enough. You don't have to choose that for yourself; you can allow yourself to make mistakes. Stop judging yourself all the time, and start being compassionate with yourself! Treat yourself the way you would treat a friend.

> *When it comes down to it, the only person who can choose your standards is you—so give yourself a break.*

I have always naturally been a perfectionist, and I've always had extremely high standards for myself. I want to do my very best in every situation, and I want people to accept me and receive me well 100 percent of the time, but I've learned that sometimes that's just not gonna happen. Especially if you do something that puts you in front of people.

Like with my outfits, for example. I always liked putting crazy things together, but as I got older, I started to compare myself to all these super-trendy girls I saw on Instagram, and I felt like I wasn't good enough because I didn't look as cool as I thought they looked. And as I started getting more popular on YouTube, a few people made some really critical comments about my outfit choices. It made me feel like I wasn't up to the standard of the "perfect" girl I'd always wanted to be. I started trying to wear simpler clothes, and I got down on myself. I lost the artistic joy I had always had in putting together outfits. Instead, I was just dressing for other people.

I would rather stay true to who I am and what feels authentic to me than look cool and trendy.

After a while, I realized I was playing this demoralizing game of comparison and perfectionism. And I didn't wanna play it anymore. When you're being yourself, you're never gonna reach crazy-high standards of perfection, because they are not human! They don't leave room for personality and art and color. I would rather stay true to who I am and what feels authentic to me than look cool and trendy.

DEALING WITH STRESS

What even *is* stress? We know it when we feel it, but when we don't know where it's coming from, we can easily let it snowball into a dramatic situation. Part of taking care of ourselves is learning to read our own feelings and respond in a healthy way to what they are telling us.

Katherine

I know this may sound unbelievable in the moment you're dealing with stress, but stress comes from a negative mind-set. For me, stress is all about living in the future—panicking that there is too much to do and you will never be able to get it done, and then your world will end. Let me tell you—that's not true! I promise, you can deal with this! You've got to take a step back and look at the big picture.

When I was dealing with a project that was completely stressing me out, one of our friends said to me, "You are going to get it done either way—stressed or relaxed—so why not just get it done without being stressed?" I know: *way* easier said than done, but good to keep in mind.

When I feel overwhelmed, making a to-do list always makes me feel better. Sometimes, the worst part is simply this foreboding feeling that you're not sure what needs to get done, but you know it's a lot. It's that Terror of Not Knowing. But sometimes when you write it down, you'll realize it's not as much as you thought it would be. Break things down into baby steps—the smaller the better. And please reward yourself with something special when you're done!

⋯⋯⋯ ★ KATHERINE'S TO-DO LIST ★ ⋯⋯⋯

SATURDAY, MARCH 2

- Laundry: wash, dry, fold, and put away
- Make grocery list (get ideas from Pinterest for 1–2 new meals)
- Get groceries
- Prep meals for week

- Take some time to relax! Read, write, or color. Do NOT get on phone for at least 1–2 hours!
- Call Sarah after lunch
- Exercise for 30 minutes. Walk? (Check weather)
- Plan out budget for the month

Lauren

Everyone gets stressed and anxious, and it can really mess with your life. But no matter how bad it is, don't let stress and anxiety stop you from doing things you want and need to do! Just take it one thing at a time. Do what you need to do *right now*, and then when you're done with that, do the next thing. Making a list is a great idea; and I'd add prioritizing that list so you can do the most important things first. Let go of trying to get everything done all the time. 'Cause sometimes you just can't. And that's okay!

If you're stressed about the future, try talking rationally to yourself. "What is the worst thing that could happen?" You probably won't die, so calm down and let yourself live!

Lisa

If you know you're in a stressful place, try hanging up some affirming messages on your bathroom wall so you have a daily reminder that life really isn't as hard as you feel like it is. Everything is going to be okay—eventually.

Just think: in ten years, what you're stressing about right now probably won't matter. Do you *really* think that when you're twenty-seven and living your life, you'll be thinking about the paper you got a B on ten years ago? No, you won't, 'cause that's stupid. I'd say 99 percent of the stuff we worry about is not *that* life changing or important in the grand scheme of things.

And as for things that *are* life changing and important, stressing about them *still* isn't going to help you make a good decision. Remember that even this difficult time period won't last forever. When my sisters and I were deciding whether to leave our record deal behind and start over in a brand-new state, I felt paralyzed. The thought of leaving all my friends behind, leaving my state behind, leaving the security of our jobs, and taking on all the responsibility of our livelihood was terrifying. But our parents raised us to be risk-takers and to believe in the possibility of our future. We knew we could handle it even though it was really scary. We took the plunge and pushed forward, and I'm happy to say it was quite possibly the best decision we ever made. So hang in there. Don't let fear take over. God has a plan for all of us that we can't always see, but if we keep walking forward and ask for guidance with every step, we will not be left to figure it out alone.

Just think: in ten years, what you're stressing about right now probably won't matter.

HOW TO SURVIVE AN EMOTIONAL BREAKDOWN

Your emotions are not your enemy. But they sure can feel like it sometimes. Whether it's an emotional storm brought on by stress, a particular event, or just the fact that life is hard, know that you have what it takes to get through to the other side—and you'll get to know yourself in the process. You can take back control!

Your emotions are not your enemy. But they sure can feel like it sometimes.

7

Christina

I am very experienced in the area of emotional breakdowns. I'm not using that as a medical term, and of course I'm not a doctor. That's what I call those times when you're so overwhelmed with negative emotions that you just can't function normally, like when a car overheats and quits working. I've been through periods of my life where they came weekly, and sometimes even daily. The thing about emotional breakdowns is that they generally have the same beginning, middle, and end. They're pretty predictable. That means you can know what to expect and talk yourself through each phase. Let's go through them.

THE BEGINNING

You can feel it happening. You're starting to freak out. It's all piling on at once, and you're feeling out of control. In this stage, just be aware that you're starting to have an emotional breakdown and admit it to yourself. You have to do this before you can start to get a game plan together for how you're going to get through it. See if you can identify what triggered the freak-out, and name how you're feeling about it.

THE MIDDLE

This is the messier part. You might start to feel hopeless. You don't know when this will end. What I like to do is get it all out: express all the emotions in a journal, to a friend, on a walk listening to dramatic songs, or whatever I need to do. Express it; get it out there—let it be known that you're struggling. Ask for support. Ask for advice, collect it, but you get to decide if you want to follow that advice. Sometimes I've ended up not following advice I asked for, but it was just nice to hear that people care, and they tried!

Usually during The Middle, you'll realize you are freaking out about something in one of two categories. With one kind, you'll have a solid and clear next step. (For instance, "I'm so stressed I have so much homework I can't do this I'm a failure my life is over" clearly needs to be followed by tackling the homework and finishing all that needs to be done.) But with the other kind of emotional breakdown, you might not be able to pinpoint what it's about. When you're agonizing over thoughts like *I don't know if this guy is right for me* or *Is this the college I should go to?* you can't quite "logic" your way out of it! You make your pro/con list and do your best, but it doesn't always have a clear and obvious next step to take.

This is tough, but still fixable. Start with taking things one day at a time and commit to heading in a certain direction for the time being (but not necessarily permanently)—like talking things through with that guy or visiting and interviewing people at the college. Taking action, however small, will help you end your breakdown because you'll be moving again and progressing in some way.

This brings me to the main goal of The Middle: create your strategy.

1. Make a list of what you're going to do in an attempt to solve your problems, or at least get moving in a certain direction instead of standing still.
2. Make a separate list of what self-care and positive message-related things you're going to do for yourself to help power through. These may include:

- taking a relaxing bath while listening to uplifting music
- going on a relaxing night walk

- journaling with candles and soft music playing
- painting your nails
- doing a face mask
- deep cleaning your room and bathroom

Expressing yourself and making a plan can get your mind on a new, positive track. Then you move on to "The End."

THE END

Now you implement your plan, start moving, and see yourself going somewhere other than where you were stuck before. Your mood will lift because you'll realize you are in a different place now. You're a bit more relaxed because you just took care of yourself, and you're thinking more positively because you took real, intentional actions toward getting to a more positive place.

It feels great to realize you pulled out of that rough emotional breakdown! You also gained knowledge for the future and confidence in knowing that you *can* get through rough times. So give yourself some credit! You've gotta be your own biggest supporter. You deserve it and need it.

DEALING WITH ANXIETY

Anxiety is a feeling often tinged with overwhelming nervousness and fear. While we all feel anxious sometimes, dealing with the condition of anxiety and panic attacks requires special care. Again, we aren't doctors (and it might be a good idea to see one or talk to your parents if you're suffering from crippling anxiety), but we want you to know that this is a problem that can be dealt with, and you are not alone!

Have no anxiety at all, but in everything, by prayer and petition, with thanksgiving, make your requests known to God. Then the peace of God that surpasses all understanding will guard your hearts and minds in Christ Jesus.

PHILIPPIANS 4:6-7

Katherine

I have struggled with anxiety and panic attacks since I was a kid. I have never experienced anything more terrifying than a panic attack—it makes me feel like I am literally about to die. Stomachaches, shaking hands, a pounding heart, and sleepless nights . . . It's been a lifelong struggle for me, and something I'm still trying to figure out.

I can usually trace my attacks back to something triggering me and my body responding. This looks like my heart beating fast, my stomach twisting into a knot, and overall this sinking feeling that something dreadful is happening. The scary part is, I don't even notice it at first. I just have this feeling of, *My life is over. I will never be happy again.* It all seems so logical and rational to feel this way in the beginning. After I am able to calm down and see more clearly, I can see how my thinking was out of whack and out of touch with reality; but in the moment, darkness and doom seemed inevitable.

For me, triggers often relate to:

- a person reacting badly to me and saying something negative, and me feeling like I'm a horrible person
- a heavy workload piling up and feeling like time is slipping away quickly

- boys (*sigh!*)
- feeling ashamed and out of control about something, like money, the future, or my body

One of my greatest accomplishments in life has been learning how to sit and breathe through a panic attack. I can now figure out pretty quickly when it is happening, and I usually sit down and start crying to try to help release the pent-up emotion. I'll cry as hard and as long as I need to—sometimes for hours—and my eyes will get all swollen and puffy. If I'm able to, I'll start writing down everything I'm thinking and feeling. At first, all feels dark and hopeless, but if I cry out to God and ask for help, the light starts breaking through pretty quickly. God is great!

> I will cry to God Most High, to God who accomplishes all things for me.
>
> PSALM 57:2

I have a tendency to totally withdraw and feel paralyzed when I'm experiencing a panic attack, and it feels like reaching out would be impossible. But I would highly encourage you to reach out to a trusted, positive person when you experience moments like this. We shouldn't have to carry our burdens alone.

If you experience anxiety, depression, or anything similar, I highly recommend going to counseling.

When I was twenty, I started going to a counselor for my anxiety. My only regret is that I didn't go sooner. I have had a few different counselors over the years, and I've realized that sometimes it takes a few tries to get the right fit. Through counseling I learned so much about myself, and I was able to identify so many negative patterns that were causing my anxiety to spiral out of control. If you experience anxiety, depression, or anything similar, I highly recommend going to counseling. It is life changing when you connect with the right counselor. My advice is to give yourself grace and time and take it slow.

NURTURING THE POSITIVE

With all the emotional battles you have to go through in life, you've got to take care of yourself! It's not only about getting through the hard times—it's about savoring the good times too. You are a unique, one-of-a-kind creation, and it isn't conceited or vain to acknowledge that and take care of the "you" God gave you. It's true what people say about putting on your own oxygen mask before putting on someone else's, like in those airplane safety demonstrations. Giving yourself what you need makes you not only a happy, healthy human being but someone who is able to help others too. When it comes to taking care of yourself, there's so much you can do.

You are an amazing creation, and it isn't vain or selfish to acknowledge that and take care of the "you" God gave you.

NURTURING ACTIVITIES TO TRY

Lisa

Every time I get stressed-out, the only thing that makes me feel better without fail is doing something to nurture myself. I think of these things instinctively. Without even trying to, I start craving a warm bath or a new manicure. You won't believe what a difference little things can make. Here are some things you can do to nurture yourself:

- Go to the gym or exercise
- Paint your nails
- Do a hair mask (even plain coconut oil is great)
- Write in a journal
- Call a friend and specifically talk about what's going on in your mind—conversation can be healing!
- Stretch
- Clean your room
- Clean your bathroom
- Organize your closet
- Listen to calming music that expresses whatever is going on inside of you
- Eat healthy food
- Write a song or poem about what you're feeling/ thinking
- Hang out with your pet if you have one (animals can take stress levels down big-time)
- Sit outside alone and breathe—take in nature

Katherine

For a recovering people pleaser like me, it has been extremely hard to learn to prioritize self-care, but once you do, you may be surprised at how much easier it is to love yourself and your body. Here is what has been helpful for me:

- Take care of your hygiene. I am really big on this! Keeping yourself clean is a very loving thing to do for your body—simple but effective. After a bath I like to mix lotion with coconut oil and put it on slowly. Appreciate your beautiful body and all the amazing things it can do!
- Drink lots of water every day, and *do not sleep in your makeup*. Please. For the love of your skin. Wash your face and put on moisturizer before bed. You will thank yourself for it!
- Light candles and listen to soothing music. I like to pray and meditate with candles during my most stressful moments, and without fail, it always calms me.
- Give yourself a hug, and whisper kind words to yourself. I know that sounds cheesy, but I promise it works! Sometimes when I'm lying in bed, I'll close my eyes and repeat positive phrases, such as "I am healthy. I am safe. I am grateful. I am at peace." It makes me feel so good!
- Do art projects or color. I like to put on playlists of songs I love and make collages or draw abstract drawings with colored pencils. Use that time to think deeply about life and dream!

START A GRATITUDE JOURNAL

In all circumstances give thanks, for this is the will of God for you in Christ Jesus.

1 THESSALONIANS 5:18

Christina

Gratitude journaling is one of the simplest yet most powerful things you can do to improve your life. It's hard to imagine that something so easy could have such a huge impact, but I have seen it transform people's lives—my own included.

After writing in their gratitude journals daily for several days, many people have experienced a crazy and random kind of "bliss" out of nowhere. They will be going throughout their day and then randomly get really happy for no reason. This is a common side effect of being grateful, and one reason I highly recommend it.

Not sure how to begin? No worries—I'm going to tell you exactly how you can start to journal your gratitude.

Start by choosing a notebook or journal. This can be any notebook you have. You can even decorate it and make it fun. It's also nice to have some good pens, markers, or colored pencils in case you feel like getting creative. There is no right or wrong way to gratitude journal. But I've noticed that this way has been very effective for me:

1. Do not simply write out a random list of things you are grateful for. Instead, write out something along the lines of "I am so very grateful that . . ."
2. Then write out, "THANK YOU!" a few times until you are really aware that you are grateful for what you've written.

If you're not sure what to write, think about these categories to get you started:

- friends
- relationships
- family
- finances
- school

- your home
- health
- talents

You don't have to be in a 100 percent perfect place to have something to be grateful for. You may have major health problems in one part of your body, but maybe you still have two perfectly working legs. You could be *very* grateful for what you do have!

Try gratitude journaling for just one week, and really push yourself to *feel* the gratitude. I think the results will be motivation enough to continue!

Amy

Gratitude journaling has made such an impact on my life. I started doing it, and it made my day so much better. You could even do it on your phone or computer.

When I started gratitude journaling, every morning I would write out five things I was grateful for—five blessings I could see no matter how bad my day was going. These could be as simple as "I am thankful for nail polish," or as abstract as "I am thankful for love and guidance from You, Lord."

There is always something to be grateful for.

Gratitude journaling has shifted my focus to looking for things that I could be grateful for throughout the day. It got me out of the negative mind-set of focusing on only what is wrong with my life. It got me to focus on all the good things I already have! The smallest things can make a *big* difference. Try it and see what happens. There is *always* something to be grateful for.

17

A BEAUTIFUL RELATIONSHIP WITH YOURSELF

Where do you think you'll be ten years from now? What do you hope your relationship with yourself will be like? We hope it will be forgiving, loving, nurturing, and full of the peace that comes from taking care of yourself. Things will be hard, no doubt, but we hope you will learn to go easy on yourself, be gentle with yourself, and even laugh at yourself from time to time.

Sometimes we wish we could go back in time and give ourselves some advice and encouragement—to understand the importance of building a strong, healthy self-relationship. (In fact, at the end of this book, you'll find some letters we wrote our younger selves with things we wished we'd known about everything we'll talk about in this book.)

Remember that everything you'll face in life is affected by the attitude you have toward yourself. As you read on, we hope you'll keep reflecting on the fact that you are a beautiful, valuable work in progress—and worth investing in.

> I praise you, because I am wonderfully made; wonderful are your works! My very self you know.
> PSALM 139:14

JOURNAL

- Think of a time you tend to get stressed or anxious. What can you do to make a game plan so you can handle what life throws at you?
- How do you tend to hold yourself to an impossibly high

standard? Take a minute to think about where you got these over-the-top ideas, and write a letter to yourself, giving yourself permission to be YOU instead.

• Make a commitment to writing in a gratitude journal every day this week, even if it's just a few things. Then reflect: how did this change your outlook on life?

PRAY

God, thank You for making me who You made me to be. Help me enjoy the life You have given me and treat this mind, body, and heart with love and care, today and every day. Thank You for loving me! Please be with me as I learn to love myself, grow through my struggles, and celebrate how uniquely You have made me.

CHAPTER 2

SPIRITUALITY

WHO IS GOD TO YOU? Spirituality is an incredibly sensitive, personal topic. Every person, no matter his or her beliefs, at one point has to answer the question, What do you believe in? Even if you don't have a relationship with God currently, the way you answer that question will define a huge part of your life. A relationship with God isn't simply "going to church." It's so much deeper. We can't talk about taking care of ourselves without talking about our spirituality, because we're not just mind and body, but a soul too!

We are a Catholic family, and we were raised by a mom who is deeply passionate about her faith. She wove Christian teaching into the homeschooling curriculum she designed for us, and from a young age we absorbed Christian values into our core identities. Although we are far from perfect, our faith has been the guiding principle to keep us on track in life.

After we moved to Los Angeles when most of us were teenagers, we experienced a lot of pushback from the entertainment industry for our values. Pressure came from our record label, from stylists, and from music industry professionals who told us we needed to conform

Although we are far from perfect, our faith has been the guiding principle to keep us on track in life.

to the industry's values by dressing more risqué, singing songs with messages that went against our values, and conforming to the notion that women need to be sexualized to have success in the music industry.

The immense pressure and constant trials drained us to the core. After five years, we were sick of it and on the verge of quitting music. Luckily, we moved to Nashville at just the right moment, and everything changed for us! With full creative control, we became a lot more positive and reenergized about making music and creating content. The common thread and core of our message came from our faith in God. Without our faith, we would not be who we are in every way. It literally informs everything we do.

In this chapter, we want to start sharing with you who God is to us. And because we know a relationship with Him is so important, we'll talk about getting closer to God through prayer and developing a personal relationship with Him as well as connecting with people and sharing faith with those who don't share the faith. God tells us, "You will seek Me and find Me when you search for Me with all your heart." (Jeremiah 29:13).

WHO IS GOD TO ME?

No matter where you are on the religion and spirituality scale, from "very spiritual" to "not at all," you probably have your own ideas about who God is or isn't. We think the best way to start thinking about your spiritual self is answering the question, "Who is God to me?" Here's how we'd answer.

Dani

God is my rock. He is always there, even when I can't feel Him. He is constant; He is love; He is forever within me.

I realize that God gives us everything we could ever need, but sometimes I don't even appreciate it. I take so much for granted every day, but I should be waking up and seeing those beautiful pink flowers outside my window that the Lord blessed us with and thanking Him for that.

God is someone who loves me more than anyone else on earth does, but He is someone I struggle to love. Loving Him is a conscious decision I have to make. Praying, reading, and living out His Word is such a hard thing for me to do sometimes, but it's worth it. There are times I don't always *feel* He is there, but I always *know* He is. It's crazy, because we can't see Him, but somehow I feel more whole than ever when I feel close with Him.

I cannot describe how I got here, or how He created a whole universe, but I can describe the feeling of security I get from Him. It doesn't last forever, because I am only human, but the times when I am praying, reading the Bible, listening in Mass, and doing all the things I love are the times I know I'm exactly where I'm supposed to be.

Lisa

When I think of God, I think of an understanding Father. I think of someone who cares and hears me and wants good things for me. I've never seen Him as a mean, judgmental dude who's gonna strike me down at any second or some invisible being that doesn't care. I've felt His presence before, definitely.

I was at my uncle's house on a warm July night in 2011, and I was outside, lying on their trampoline. The sun had just set, so it was still a little light, but I could see a lot of stars coming out. I was listening to positive songs on my iPod about what's important in life and how I'll never need more than what I have. I felt so grateful and happy to be alive, regardless of what was going right or wrong in my life. For the first time (I think ever), I started to cry tears of joy.

When I think of God, I think of an understanding Father.

I felt God all around me in that moment. And that's what God is to me: peace. He's an overwhelming sense of joy, a safe place. I don't have to be perfect, because I am accepted, appreciated, wanted, cherished, and loved by Him at all times, regardless of what I'm going through. God truly is love.

The less I worry about worldly things (money, my looks, what people think of me, competing with others, comparing myself, work, things like that) and the more I focus my brain on loving myself and the people around me and just appreciating each simple moment, the more connected to God I feel.

The peace of God that surpasses all understanding will guard your hearts and minds in Christ Jesus.

PHILIPPIANS 4:7

Christina

God is my source of peace, strength, and light. Simply put, God is love. When I broke down and finally admitted to myself that I cannot in fact carry the weight of the world on my shoulders alone, God stepped in for me and gave me strength to ask for help. God is a warm feeling of peace washing over me. He's a light guiding my every step. He is love enveloping me when I need it most. God guides me, protects me, carries me, calms me, and loves me. He warns me, nudges me, redirects me, and sometimes keeps things from me. He is hope. He is more than our human conception of Him. He is the one thing above all that grounds me and gives me life. I know that no matter what happens in my life, I can always look to Him for guidance, peace, and love. With Him, I am accepted. I am fully known. I am loved regardless of my mistakes or my flaws. I don't have to pretend or try to be anything with God. He is unconditional love. Ultimate acceptance. Radical mercy. God is a never-ending, life-giving source for me. He is my anchor. A fount of love. God is the one ever-present, constant, and unchanging thing in this ever-changing and unsteady world.

God is my source of peace, strength, and light. Simply put, God is love.

Lauren

God is the realist homie on the block. Haha. But for real . . . you could literally reject Him and insult Him and hate Him, but He would never stop loving you. God is really the only one I know I can count on. When everything is chaotic and horrible and constantly changing, He is the same. He will always love me no matter what. Sometimes I don't understand why He loves me, because I am definitely not a perfect person. I go through a lot of spiritual down times where I feel very disconnected from Him. But every time I think I can get through things on my

I want God to speak and live through me, and I want my life to bring glory to Him.

25

own and I don't need Him or anyone else, I am always proved wrong. I cannot survive and thrive without Him; it is impossible. He is a comfort and refuge in a world where those things don't even seem to exist. When I am able to let go of my pride and give Him control of my life, I am always amazed at how good He is. He wants the best for me and for every one of His children.

A lot of times I don't understand why He lets things happen the way they do or why He made me the way I am, but I don't know how I could ever expect to understand the Creator of the universe when I don't even understand the universe He created. I want Him to be pulling my strings. I want Him to speak and live through me, and I want my life to bring glory to Him.

Amy

When I think of God, I think of a protector. I think of a guiding light that's always got my best interests at heart. God is the one thing that keeps me grounded; when everything is feeling out of control, I can look to Him to have my back. Knowing that He is there for me brings me so much peace. Even if I feel like nobody is there for me in the entire world, I can take comfort knowing that He is.

[God] is the Giver, and I have had to learn how to let myself receive all He has for me!

God is my very beginning and everything up until the ultimate end. His love and direction give my life purpose and stability. I know He will always be there. I feel closest to Him when I am empty and broken and searching for His light, but also when I am overflowing with love and gratitude. I feel His presence when I'm in nature, while I am watching the sun set, or even when walking near a beautiful field.

To me, He is the reason for my life. He is the Giver, and I have had to learn how to let myself receive all He has for me! I firmly believe that God feels different to all of us. I believe we all have different views and experiences in how we relate to Him. How I relate to Him is going to be totally different from how anyone else relates to Him because we all have completely different life experiences that shape how we view Him. Remember that. Explore who He is, and He will reveal Himself to you! All you have to do is ask Him to meet you halfway.

> God is our refuge and strength, an ever-present help in distress.
>
> PSALM 46:2

Katherine

I remember first having an awareness of God when I was twelve. I experienced Him as a warm, love-light Being who loved and cared for me very much. As I struggled with insecurity, anxiety, family problems, self-esteem, and identity, I knew in the back of my mind that the Creator was present with me and I could come to Him as a safe place to rest.

I didn't begin to understand God on a deeper level until I was seventeen. This was when I began having very real, personal encounters with Him. These experiences came during prayer, when I would feel totally washed in His love and freed from the usual constraints of my mind—anxiety, fear, and judgment of myself. For a few brief moments during these encounters, I could see myself as God created me—flawed but lovable. Not the best, not the worst, yet infinitely important and somehow *precious* to this omnipotent Being.

When I experience God, there is no greater feeling. It is a definite knowing that all will be well—complete peace.

When I experience God, there is no greater feeling. It is a definite knowing that all will be well—complete peace. It is an overwhelming, powerful feeling of love for all people—a tidal wave of compassion. It is being washed clean from sin, guilt, and shame—exhilarating freedom. To this day, nothing on earth has compared to the intense joy and fulfillment I have experienced with God.

PRAYER: HAVING A CONVERSATION WITH GOD

We've learned that the best way to start praying is just to start. Just do it, even if it feels awkward, and know that God isn't judging you by how eloquent or "perfect" your prayer is. He really just wants to hear from you. Here's how prayer plays a part in our lives.

Lauren

I've learned the most important thing is to be honest. If you're not being honest with God, it's kind of pointless to pray—especially since He already knows what you're thinking and how you're feeling.

Okay, so if He already knows, why do I need to tell Him? Because it's about connecting with Him and making Him a part of your life. How do you do that? It's the same thing you do with your friends. You tell them about yourself and how your day was and what's going on with you (even if sometimes they already know these things). You talk to them regularly. You tell them how you appreciate having them in your life. You express your gratitude to them. If they're a really big part of your life, you have them in the back (or front) of your mind most of the day.

That's how it should be with prayer.

Give yourself some time before you go to sleep to tell God about your day. Tell Him how you felt about everything that happened and what you were grateful for. Ask Him your questions and tell Him your thoughts. Tell Him you love Him if you feel like it. If you're mad, tell Him what you're mad about. If you need help with something, ask Him.

I have the tendency to be a people pleaser and to try to appear perfect to everyone; so sometimes it's hard for me to be honest in prayer because I think, *I'm not perfect. I sin and offend Him, like, every day, so why would He even want to talk to me?* He wants to because He *loves us.* He knows we're not perfect and we never will be. All He wants is for us to try our best and to love Him.

Amy

Prayer is the root of our relationship with God. In my experience, I've found it's important to be fully focused when I pray. God doesn't require your whole day, just your full attention! Remember: God knows you deeper than anyone. He will never reject you, and He's the best listener!

Meditation is another amazing way to pray. Clear your mind and focus on your breathing. Repeat a phrase or verse from Scripture, and really focus on it. There are all sorts of beautiful practices that help us in our prayer life. For instance, I love praying the Rosary, a Catholic practice. It centers me and calms me down. It's also helpful when I can't sleep!

God knows you deeper than anyone. He will never reject you, and He's the best listener!

Explore your mind and your relationship with God. Anytime you use a skill or talent He gave you, it's an opportunity to connect with Him. You are praising Him and enjoying all He has given you. Prayer is different for all of us, so try out different things until you figure out what you connect with most.

GETTING CLOSER TO GOD

In addition to prayer, here are a few more things we do to get closer to God. These habits bring strength and clarity to our souls, build us up, and make us stronger in our faith.

Christina

In my experience, getting closer to God is all about developing daily habits. As with friendships, you need to put in daily effort if you want your relationship with God to grow. This concept seems almost too simple, but if you apply it in your own life, you will see what I mean.

On top of daily prayer, here are some habits that could help you develop a closer relationship with God:

LISTENING

Set aside time, even if it's just a few moments, to listen to God. This can be on a walk, sitting in your bed, or anywhere, really. Just make the effort to be in silence for a moment and ask God to speak to you as a part of your prayer time. Open your heart up to His voice and see what He has to say.

God gave us the Bible so we could learn about Him. And we have not only this but whole libraries of books by wise people who tell us about Him and about their own experiences with God. Look around for a subject you're interested in that has to do with God, and choose a book about it. You don't have to read a whole book every week or anything crazy; just start out with creating a daily ritual of reading, for instance, five pages before bed. The practice of doing it every day will make a big impact.

········ ⭐ SOME OF OUR FAVORITE ⭐ ········ SPIRITUAL BOOKS

Mere Christianity and *The Screwtape Letters* by C. S. Lewis
Time for God and *Searching for and Maintaining Peace* by
    Jacques Philippe
Help, Thanks, Wow: The Three Essential Prayers by Anne
    Lamott
Captivating by John and Stasi Eldredge
Man's Search for Meaning by Viktor Frankl
The Interior Castle by Saint Teresa of Ávila
The Robe by Lloyd C. Douglas[1]

WATCHING YOUTUBE VIDEOS OF PEOPLE SHARING THEIR FAITH OR LISTENING TO BOOKS ON TAPE

This is another easy one. I do this in the morning when I'm making breakfast or while I'm cleaning or doing laundry. It's so simple to just turn on the wisdom, listen, and get something else done at the same time.

MUSIC

Listening to praise and worship music (or any songs that make you feel connected to God) is not only fun but also very effective in strengthening your relationship with Him. I've made this a daily habit by listening to Christian music when I shower. Making it a part of another daily habit is a great way to help it stick.

········ ★ OUR FAVORITE WORSHIP ★ ········ MUSIC PLAYLIST

"You Say" by Lauren Daigle
"Maybe It's OK" by We Are Messengers
"Thy Will" by Hillary Scott and the Scott Family
"I Love You, Lord" by Matt Maher
"Speak Life" by TobyMac
"Need You More" by For King & Country
"Fearless" by Jasmine Murray
"O God Forgive Us" by For King & Country
"King of My Heart" by Bethel Music (the Kutless version is
    awesome too!)
"How He Loves" by David Crowder Band
"Pieces" by Amanda Cook
"I Shall Not Want" by Audrey Assad
"Let Your Love Be Strong" by Switchfoot
"I Won't Let You Go" by Switchfoot
"Hills and Valleys" by Tauren Wells
"I Don't Wanna Go" by Chris Renzema

"Little Girl" by His Own
"No Longer Slaves" by Bethel Music

Katherine

Something I've learned the last several years is *not* to base my relationship with God on emotional highs. The truth is, in your walk with Him, you will experience many ups and downs.

Encountering a season of spiritual dryness (a time when you don't really feel God's presence) does *not* necessarily mean you did anything wrong. It espe-
cially does not mean you should give up on God—but even if you did, He would never give up on you. Your relationship with God grows through a commitment, and commitment cannot be based in feelings. Feelings come

> *Something I've learned the last several years is not to base my relationship with God on emotional highs.*

and go. But commitments are steadfast and devoted to enduring all seasons of life together.

Here are some of the things that have been really helpful for me in getting closer to God.

A DEDICATED MORNING ROUTINE

This is the one thing in my life that has made the biggest dif-ference. Every morning I read the daily Catholic Scripture readings (you can read whatever works for your faith tradition), write in my prayer journal, and read from a devotional. I can't stress enough how much this has affected my life!

One day after I had recently recommitted to this practice, I noticed I was feeling much more anxious and negative. *Wow! What is so remarkably different with me today?* I thought. Then I realized I hadn't done my morning routine that day!

PRAYER JOURNALING

There is something powerful about writing down prayers. For me, I think it's because I get so distracted and my mind is pretty jumbled, so writing helps me focus. Try it for a few minutes each morning or night and see if it helps you!

LISTENING TO SONGS ABOUT GOD

As a musician, I know how much music can affect your mood and your outlook. And it can be an important part of your walk with God! I listen to a variety of worship songs, from old Gregorian chant, to traditional Catholic hymns like "O Salutaris Hostia," to contemporary Christian music. It always uplifts me and brightens my day!

READING SCRIPTURE

Studying the Bible is one of the best ways to get closer to God, simply because it helps you learn about who He is and what His character is like. I love doing Bible studies, and sometimes I'll randomly think of something, such as, *What does the Bible say about angels?* or, *I wonder what the Gospels say about Jesus' crucifixion?* Then I'll read the Scriptures, think them through, and ask God to guide me toward whatever truth He wants to reveal.

Sometimes you get clogged up. Things get in the way. Life gets crazy, schedules get hectic, and the next thing you know, you haven't prayed in a week. Some of us haven't prayed in a month, a year, or at all. Even when life is crazy, though, we can take steps to get our priorities straight.

Think of all the things you do in a day that don't actually benefit you much. What do you do each day that *actually improves* your life? You can try taking back control of wasted time by taking yourself on a mini spiritual retreat. Choose a place where you'll be alone long enough to empty your mind. This is where you find God—in the silence. Find a quiet place and listen to God. Drive somewhere, if you need to, to get away from it all. Pray. Take some time to clear out your head and get in touch with God. List all the things you're grateful for, and think of all the things you need help with. Sit there and just try to feel thankful that you're alive.

Do this regularly. Talk to God. Tell Him all the things you're too scared to talk to other people about. He will listen.

THE POWER OF COMMUNITY

Faith is beautiful when we're on our own, quietly praying and spending time with God, but it can be so powerful when we meet with others to worship, pray, learn, and come together as a community. Here are some of our experiences of coming together with others and how community has strengthened our faith journeys.

Katherine

When I lived in California, it was very rare to find friends who shared my Catholic faith. I had a couple of friends who were

You can try taking back control of wasted time by taking yourself on a mini spiritual retreat.

Catholic, and occasionally I went to young adult groups, but they were so far away from my house I rarely went.

When I moved to Nashville, it was the first time I was ever surrounded by a strong community of people who shared my faith, and it was the most amazing experience. My faith shot to a whole new level as I made friends with groups of people who not only loved their faith but lived it out together. Some would host worship nights at their house. Some started Bible studies and small groups. Some of us would attend Adoration together, which is a Catholic form of prayer.

From my experience, having a group of friends who are strong in their faith will change your life and strengthen your faith. I strongly encourage you to do whatever you can to find these people! To this day, they are some of my truest, most inspiring friends.

Amy

Praying with and for other people is one of the most powerful gifts we can give. It's so important to share our struggles and to lean on each other to lift us up to our Father. That said, it can be kinda awkward to ask others to pray for us. I know I don't do it nearly as much as I should—and when I do, usually it's when I'm in deep times of crisis.

Once, when I was going through a medical issue, I was feeling so small and defeated. So I went through my phone book, and I asked everyone I knew to pray for me. I did the same thing when my friend was facing a serious illness. I literally texted and Facebook messaged

I want to be able to share my struggles with my community of friends and know that they will lift me up in prayer.

everyone I knew who believed in God and asked them to pray for her. It was awkward at first, but I truly believe these prayers made a difference, and we felt so supported and loved. I want to be able to share my struggles with my community of friends and know that they will lift me up in prayer. That is what truly builds a community of God.

Christina

I distinctly remember a time in my life when my romantic relationship with my then boyfriend, now husband, Nick, was greatly suffering. I was living in turmoil and making mistake after mistake, watching our relationship crumble and feeling powerless to fix it. I felt isolated, lonely, ashamed, confused, and frequently pretty miserable about it. At one point, a strong feeling of peace came over me, and I knew in my heart that someone was praying for my relationship. I didn't quite know how I knew—I just knew. My heart started to change, and I saw my relationship rapidly shift into an incredibly positive place. When I shared this with my sisters, Katherine told me she had been fervently praying for me that entire time! I was shocked and yet not at all surprised because I knew that was what I had been feeling. Prayer makes an incredible difference, especially when we do it in community!

FAITH IN ACTION

You've heard that actions speak louder than words. People tend to think of faith as a mental thing. It's just as important to *act out* our love for God and for people in the real world.

Katherine

When I think about faith in action, I think about service. Jesus was extremely clear in His teaching that we are called to take care of people, especially the poor and vulnerable. There are so many ways to do this!

You can volunteer at a soup kitchen, organize a food drive, or help out at any nonprofit in your area that serves those in need. Also, don't forget some of the more "ordinary" situations where you can practice charity in your daily life: for instance, babysitting for free for a family that needs help, or even reaching out to a kid in your class who is isolated and lonely. We are called to be the hands and feet of Christ, which means to treat others with extraordinary love, mercy, and compassion, like He did!

We are called to be the hands and feet of Christ, which means to treat others with extraordinary love, mercy, and compassion, like He did!

I started volunteering when I was a kid, and I always loved it. It made me feel purposeful and alive, as if I was doing the most powerful thing with my time. If you feel empty, like your life might be missing something, it could very possibly be service!

Dani

Growing up, I thought the only way you could serve others was by going on a mission trip to Africa and feeding children. While that is a wonderful way to help, not all acts of service are so major. Nowadays, I like to think of little ways I can make the lives around me better, and that is my main way of serving. For example, offering to walk my sister's new dog when she's pressed for time, or getting up to get something for a sibling when I really just feel like sitting on the couch. Making little things like this part of your mind-set is a way of serving others. It's not dramatic, but it can become a way of life. Most of us in this world aren't millionaires, missionaries, or celebrities. We can't really make huge, publicized changes that impact hundreds of people at a time, but we can make a difference to people in our lives bit by bit.

Lisa

I believe that serving other people truly brings meaning to a person's life. If everything you do is all about what *you* want and how *you* can get yourself ahead, you can quickly start to feel like you have no purpose. But we all have a purpose, and it's generally so much easier to find it when you're using your time to help someone else.

> *We all have a purpose, and it's generally so much easier to find it when you're using your time to help someone else.*

JOURNAL

- Who is God to you? Write out your impressions of God and where you think they came from.
- To make prayer a more regular part of your life, consider keeping a prayer list in your prayer journal. Bullet point a few things you are praying for yourself, for others, for the

world, and in thankfulness. Then keep track of them over time to see how God answers!

• Plan out a spiritual routine for the week. Plan out a ten- or fifteen-minute routine each day to try a few of the practices we discussed. Stick with it, and journal about what happens.

PRAY

Lord, I want to know You better. Show me how to find You in my days, and guide me as I try out new ways to get to know You. Thank You for Your promise that when I seek You, I'll find You.

CHAPTER 3
FRIENDSHIP

FINDING TRUE FRIENDSHIPS AND LEARNING how to keep them alive and healthy is one of the most meaningful experiences a person can have. On the flip side, dealing with a toxic or hurtful friend can be one of the most devastating. We have experienced both. We have laughed and cried with our friends, stayed up all night talking, had random glow stick dance parties with our friends, and also been rejected, betrayed, and abandoned by friends we trusted. Friendship can be a roller coaster, and just like dating, sometimes it's so painful we end up questioning it, asking ourselves, *Is it all worth it?*

When you haven't experienced true friendship, it's easy to hold on to bad friends who drive you deeper into insecurity, gossip, and drama. We wrote this chapter to give you some tools to recognize when you've found a great friendship, learn how to be a true friend, and recognize when to let a friendship go. It can be challenging, but in the end, we think you'll agree—it's all worth it. True friends are worth the fight.

As sisters, we have six very different, unique personalities. Lauren and Lisa can be more introverted and have struggled with coming out of their shells to meet new people and not isolate themselves out of fear. Katherine and Amy are both more outgoing and naturally make friends, while Christina and Dani are more in the middle with friendships. We have all helped each other out over the years, and we want to share some of the things we've learned together along the way.

True friends are worth the fight.

WHAT TO LOOK FOR IN A FRIEND

We don't often sit down and really think about what to look for in a friend, do we? Most of us aren't very intentional about it; we just let it happen naturally. But it's really important to think about this stuff—because if we don't know what we are looking for in a friendship, it makes it that much harder to find. Knowing what we don't want is important too; it sets us up for healthy, fulfilling friendships and helps us avoid pointless drama. So here are our top tips on choosing a friend you can trust.

Lauren

Don't just look for friends who are cool or fun or funny. That's nice and all, but when it comes down to it, you want a friend you can call when everything seems to be going wrong and you are crying on your bedroom floor. Here are some qualities to look for in good friends:

- They're loyal.
- You have similar morals.
- You share a similar viewpoint on life—or they have a more positive viewpoint on life than you have.
- They're good listeners. (You don't want to be friends with someone who just talks about him- or herself all the time and doesn't listen to you.)
- They're compassionate. (They don't spend a lot of time tearing people down, and they seem to genuinely care about other people's problems.)
- They put effort into the friendship.

Look for people who can stay up all night talking with you about your deep thoughts and dreams.

Do not settle for bad friends just because you don't want to be alone.

Do not settle for bad friends just because you don't want to be alone. Being alone is better than feeling alone because your friends are draining the life out of you!

Amy

One clue to whether someone is good friend material is how the person makes you feel. Does he or she make you feel trusted, appreciated, good about yourself? Ask yourself: "Do I feel like I have to change my personality around this person? Do I feel anxious, like I might say the wrong thing and my friend will make fun of me? Does this person talk about other people in a rude or degrading way?"

Watch out for people who instantly latch on to you. They are usually gone as fast as they came. It takes time and trust to build

When we are looking for friends or a relationship, we have the right to focus first on whether we like the person—not just whether she likes us.

a true connection with someone, so take your time! Sometimes we can get caught up in how people view us or think about us, but when we are looking for friends or a relationship, we have the right to focus first on whether we like the person—not just whether she likes us.

Christina

Remember that no one friend can be your everything. Because there are so many types of people in the world, there are also lots of different types of friends you can invite into your life. I do believe it's great to have a wide variety of friends so you don't put all the pressure on just one friend to meet all your friendship needs. Some friends I have are incredible to analyze life and really think with. Some are lighthearted and fun, and when we get together, we end up doing more adventurous things. Some are serious and focused on growth and improving their lives and the lives of those around them. These friends really push me to reconsider my life choices and see if I'm on a good path. Think about the different kinds of friends you need, and then you can start finding them!

HOW TO MAKE FRIENDS

Katherine here. I remember one night when Lauren was feeling really upset because she was struggling to make good friends. She had been through some very hurtful friendships, and it was hard for her to trust people, so I wanted her to focus on finding a friend she could truly trust. The truth is, it had to start inside her—and it does with you too. To make good friends, start from the inside out.

BE AUTHENTICALLY YOU

Christina

Opening up to people is one of the scariest but also most necessary things we will do as humans. Over the years, we have built up walls and put on masks. We weren't born like this, though. As babies and toddlers, we were all young and wild and free. We expressed ourselves and put ourselves out there. (Have you ever noticed how easily little kids make friends?) Sure, naturally some of us were quieter than others and more private or reserved, but we didn't think that it was something to be ashamed of, or that we needed to change anything about ourselves. No one had told us being ourselves wasn't okay yet. It didn't even cross our minds.

But as we get older, we go out into the world and have hurtful experiences. Naturally, we put on a mask and pretend we are someone more "acceptable," or we put up a shield to block all the pain.

Why do we do this? Maybe the idea of being rejected for who we *really* are is so painful that we decide we can't take it. Being rejected while wearing a mask would be less painful, because at least it's not really who we are. The big problem with all of this? People will be getting to know a person who isn't authentically you. So really, you're still strangers. You're not being vulnerable or close with people, and you can't make the kinds of friendships that really stick.

Don't let this be you. Ask yourself if there are any ways you're hiding from people, and then ask yourself why. Try to get to the

FRIENDSHIP

Anyone in your life who chooses to reject you when you are being authentic is not someone you need to be friends with.

root of it. Write down a list of things you do that you pretend to like, or things you say that are just not your authentic self. Then start to notice what you do in your day-to-day life to try to make people like you or to try to be some other person you know you're not. Start showing small pieces of yourself to people close to you. As you see them not rejecting you for it, you'll gain the courage and confidence to open up more.

And if they do reject you? These are not the people you want as friends. Anyone in your life who chooses to reject you when you are being authentic is not someone you need to be friends with. Keep going, and you *will* find your people. I promise.

To attract good friends:

- be who you really are
- like what you really like
- discover what your true passions are
- express this to the world, and share it with those you're close to

Amy

Are you in a friend rut? We get in ruts when we stop growing and when we stop pushing ourselves to grow. We stop trying new things and discovering fresh aspects of ourselves. This has happened to me so many times. When we get too comfortable where we are, we become hyperaware of how we have stopped. We cease to continue our journey in a meaningful way.

The only way to get out of a rut is to try new things! Start growing again. Force yourself out of the passive state, and make some contact with other humans! Real friendships can start when we engage with life.

Real friendships can start when we engage with life.

If you need to get out of a rut:

- try a new extracurricular activity at school
- volunteer somewhere new
- read a new book
- look up something you've never learned about before
- learn a new hobby

These are the things that make us into who we are! Follow your passions—and if you don't know what you are passionate about, go find it. Take chances. Make mistakes. Most important, have fun! Put yourself out there, and see how much happier and more adventurous your life gets.

Lauren

As Shia LaBeouf says, JUST DO IT!![1] Stop overthinking everything, and stop thinking everyone hates you, because I guarantee you, they don't. You have so much to offer this world and so much to offer a friend, so be confident.

But know this: if someone doesn't like you, it's okay. Not everyone has to like you, and not everyone will. But when you show your real self to people, your meant-to-be friends will

If someone doesn't like you, it's okay. Not everyone has to like you, and not everyone will.

LOVE you. They can't love the shell of you—only your real self. So say what you're thinking. Say what you're feeling. Talk about things that have hurt you and things you dream of doing in the future. Don't hold back because you think people will think you're weird (most likely they have felt the same thing at least once in their life and will relate to you on some level). Be your real self—you will never regret it!

PUT YOURSELF OUT THERE

Dani

If someone came up to me and asked, "Dani, how do I make friends?" the first and most important thing I would say is this: "You! Cannot! Make! Friends! Sitting! On! Your! Couch!"

If you have been hiding in your bedroom for the past two months, and one day you woke up from your Netflix marathon thinking, *Why don't I have any friends?* I can guarantee you the reason is that you can't make friends alone in your bedroom. I cannot stress enough that if you want to make friends, *you need to leave your house!* This is a lot easier if you attend any sort of school, because you have the opportunity to make new friends every single day of the school year. We were homeschooled, so we learned that to make friends you need to put yourself out there, and you might have to get creative.

If you want to make friends, you need to leave your house!

Here are some ideas:

- If you're religious, go to the youth group at your church. I have met some of my best friends this way; people at youth groups are almost always inviting.

- If you already have one or two good friends but want to meet more, ask them to introduce you to their friends. Mutual friends are a really good way to meet new people, and since you all know each other, you eventually form a squad.
- Find a small group of friendly looking people (or just one person) at lunch at school, and sit next to them. This is mildly terrifying because you have no idea if they're going to punch you in the face or be nice to you, but it's worth it.
- If you moved recently, convince your parent(s) to host a block party! Pro tip: ride around the neighborhood on your bike and leave invitations at the houses that have multiple cars, minivans, graduation signs on the front yard, or basketball hoops. Those are all signs of houses that have a teenager or young person living there. Another pro tip: host your block party on a Sunday night. It's more likely that people will be free that night.

Amy

One of the best pieces of friendship advice I've gotten is to figure out what kind of person you want to be friends with, then think of the things they would do, and do those things. Clubs and organizations are great for this. If you want to be friends with people

Most people are shy, but they actually want people to talk to them. So next time you see someone you wanna talk to, just say hi!

who love music, join the band or choir. If you want to befriend sporty people, join a sports team. If you want to befriend scuba divers, join a scuba diver club!

Remember that most people are shy, but they actually want people to talk to them. So next time you see someone you wanna talk to, just say hi! They will probably appreciate it. Making friends is all about courage. So feel the fear and get in there!

Say yes to life! *Say yes!* I used to be the worst hermit. I know all about that feeling of scarcity, like you'll never meet anyone you enjoy hanging out with, and you're gonna be alone forever. *It's not real.* Let go of the fear. You must first accept in your mind that you want friends and that you will do what it takes to find them. An open mind attracts opportunities! Get out of your house. Even if it's just your parents asking if you want to go to the grocery store, *say yes.* Go! Just talking to more people and having regular conversations with all different types of humans will make you feel less isolated and more connected, which will attract more friendship into your life. You never know who has a daughter or a nephew or a friend or a cousin you'd get along with. Every day is full of opportunity!

HOW TO KEEP FRIENDS

Congrats—you found someone you want to be friends with! Now how do you *be* a friend? How do you build that relationship and keep it strong?

Katherine

DON'T JUST TALK; LISTEN

One of the most healing parts of friendship is having a safe, loving place where you can open up and express yourself. Sometimes just telling a true friend about your problems can make those problems feel so much lighter! But this is a two-way street. If you are going to share a story, make sure you tell your friend how much you appreciate him or her listening, and then *ask* what's going on in their life. It feels so good to be asked. Even if your friend doesn't feel ready to open up, just being asked, "How are you really?" and knowing the person truly cares to know is such a comforting experience.

SEE THE BEST IN THEM

It's important to give your friends the benefit of the doubt and assume the best of them. If you have a naturally critical personality, and you constantly criticize your friends, they're probably going to start feeling hurt and defensive. Do your best to see the best in them and point it out. Give them genuine compliments, and speak up when you see something beautiful or good in them. Examples: "I was so impressed by the speech you gave in class today. You did such a good job!" "I'm really proud of you and all of your hard work. You're so talented." "You have the best personality, and you always make me laugh!" Be honest and generous, and express gratitude—your words can be a gift they remember for a long time.

> *It's important to give your friends the benefit of the doubt and assume the best of them.*

Through a few hard friendship experiences, I learned a lot about boundaries. For an in-depth explanation of boundaries, I recommend reading the book *Boundaries* by Henry Cloud and John Townsend.[2] Basically, keep your friendship healthy by respecting each other's yes and no. Don't guilt-trip or manipulate your friend when he or she doesn't do what you want. Controlling someone is not loving.

To find a true friend, be a true friend!

A true friendship is a loving, safe place where you can open up and be yourself; you feel loved, supported, and heard. To find a true friend, be a true friend!

> Iron is sharpened by iron; one person sharpens another.
>
> PROVERBS 27:17

Dani

All you can do to keep friends is treat them well. You can't force someone to be friends with you. If your friend is pushing you away, take a step back and look at how you've been treating him or her. If you think you have been respectful, honest, compassionate, and a good friend, maybe it's an issue on their end. It could be time to give that person space or let them go. If you haven't been doing your best to treat your friend well, maybe you need a little life adjustment. Sometimes the smallest examination of your behavior can help you realize that you just haven't been putting in enough effort. Being a good friend isn't too hard if you just treat friends how you want to be treated.

RESOLVING CONFLICT
WITH YOUR FRIENDS

Dani

If you get in a fight with a friend, what do you do? Avoiding the person or pretending you're fine doesn't solve anything. You can be brave and approach conflict in a healthy way by remembering to *calm down* and *be honest*.

Calm down. When emotions are running high, we can say things in inflammatory ways that make the situation worse and end up hurting people and causing more conflict. I calm myself down by going on a walk, taking a bath, or having some kind of relaxing alone time to bring myself back to a calm place physically, and then I work on calming myself mentally. I will call someone I trust, journal out a pro and con list, or write how I'm feeling and what happened, and then I try to get to the root of the problem. Why are you both *really* upset? It's not about who is right and who is wrong. It's about what needs to be addressed so you can reconnect.

It's not your responsibility to run yourself into the ground trying to please your friend.

Be honest. If you can't fully be honest, you can't fully address the root of the problem. When you've gotten yourself to a calm and reasonable state of mind, and then had an open and honest heart-to-heart with your friend, you've given it your best shot at resolving the conflict.

It's not your responsibility to run yourself into the ground trying to please your friend; do the best you can to resolve the conflict honestly and calmly without compromising your boundaries or values just to please. If you have a true friendship that will stand the test of time, you'll both work at making things better.

> A friend is a friend at all times, and a brother is born for the time of adversity.
>
> PROVERBS 17:17

WHEN FRIENDSHIP GOES BAD

If you find a friendship has taken a turn for the worse, there may still be a chance to save it—*but* you shouldn't feel like you've failed if it doesn't work out that way. Some friendships were meant to last only for a short period of time, and some are just plain not good for us. We've found there are some distinct signs of a toxic friendship. Being aware of them might save you some needless heartache.

Toxic friends can be very hard to spot. Sometimes it's under the surface and the person is passive-aggressive, and you start to feel crazy because they aren't doing anything outwardly to you, but you still feel upset around them, and it's hard to pinpoint exactly why.

How do you pinpoint a toxic friendship? Pay attention to your mind-set after you've spent time with the friend or

Friends can make an immeasurable difference in your life—you just wanna make sure that difference is positive!

when they text you. Pay attention to whether they talk about other people a lot and how they talk about them. If they are trashing others behind their backs, they are probably trashing you too.

You have to both be there for each other. Make sure they are not only focusing on you and your problems as a way to distract from their problems. You both need to be putting in equal effort. You should both be building each other up and helping each other to be the best people you can be. Friends can make an immeasurable difference in your life—you just wanna make sure that difference is positive!

Christina

If we are not sure of what we want in a friend, we may unknowingly be caught up in a destructive cycle of constantly being drawn to toxic friends. This happened to me as a teenager.

Although I did have some genuinely great friends, I was also attracted to friendships with a specific, unstable kind of person. You could call it a repeating pattern. I'd befriend the type of girl who would be super fun and an awesome friend in the beginning. Then, as time went on, she'd randomly stop talking to me out of nowhere—and I mean nowhere. One of them wouldn't even text back and ended everything so suddenly that I was very, very confused.

Upon reflecting on all of this, I started to see what these girls had in common: they were all scared of commitment of any type—friendship was just another

If you are constantly seeking out friends with major problems who are hurting you, maybe it's time to recognize that pattern and put an end to it!

commitment to them. It wasn't that anything went wrong in our friendship; they routinely "dropped" things and people in all aspects of life. I noticed these red flags and started to go forward with much more caution, looking out for bad signs before jumping into a new friendship.

Most people can probably look at their past friendships and identity some kind of pattern they've been unknowingly following in the friends they've chosen. I'm not saying don't be friends with anyone who has problems or who isn't perfect; that would leave you with *no one*. But if you are constantly seeking out friends with major problems who are hurting you, maybe it's time to recognize that pattern and put an end to it. After you hang out with someone, take note of how you feel, and be brutally honest with yourself. Are they draining you or refreshing you?

Here are some ways to know if your friendship is toxic:

- You always feel insecure around them.
- You never feel good enough for them.
- They literally insult you. (Even if it's "just a joke," it's not okay.)
- They physically hurt you in any way. (Again, even if it's "just a joke," it's not okay.)
- They talk bad about their other friends behind their backs to you. (As Amy said, this means they're likely doing the same to you.)
- They talk about only their life and their problems and don't listen to you when you talk about yourself.
- They have weird mood swings, and you never know when

they're gonna randomly be mad at you when you didn't even do anything.
- You feel like you can't stand up to them or tell them how you feel because you know they will get mad.

If any of these sound familiar, keep reading.

HOW TO BREAK UP WITH A FRIEND

You may be at the point where it's time to stand up for yourself and stop putting all your time and energy into a bad situation. The breakup may be for a short time, or it may be for good. Either way, we want you to know that it *is* an option, and you can do it with kindness and compassion.

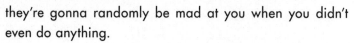

I know it's not really a common thing to "break up" with a friend, but sometimes it's necessary. Some people will think you're just being dramatic if you decide to end a friendship, but do *not* let that get to you. If a friendship is making your life worse or making you worse as a person, you need to *let it go*. It could be time to break it off if:

- they aren't treating you right
- they are living a lifestyle that is bad for them and is bad for you and you don't want to be around that anymore (for instance, they're into drinking or drugs)

If they are treating you badly, tell them about it. Tell them you're not gonna put up with it, and give them a chance to change.

Be honest and be nice, but stand firm, and don't let them make you think you are wrong or crazy for asking them to change their behavior. Then give them some time.

If they don't change their behavior in a reasonable amount of time, don't feel bad about saying, "Look, I told you it's not okay for you to treat me like that, and you continued to do it; so, sorry, but I have to respect myself and not be around people who treat me like that. Goodbye."

If you're in a situation where your friend is living a lifestyle you don't want to be a part of, you've got a couple of options. You could either slowly and politely distance yourself from them, or you could talk to them. Be like, "Hey, this thing you're doing really isn't good for you, and I don't want to be a part of it. I don't think we can continue being friends if you're gonna keep doing it, because I don't want to get into it too." If they don't change, they've made their decision.

No matter how or why you break up with a friend, never end it on a bad note.

No matter how or why you break up with a friend, never end it on a bad note. Take the high road. Don't call them any names, don't make them feel like they are a bad person, and let them know you still care about them, but this just isn't right for you. You need to respect yourself and realize you deserve to be treated with nothing less than dignity and respect in return.

Katherine

People usually break up with friends in the worst way possible, which is to just stop talking to your friend, and then it's over. I know I've done that to friends in the past and also had it done to me. Most of

58

us have been through that, and it's the *worst*. So many unanswered questions! To me the best way to break up with a friend is to have a frank talk. Talk it out! Sometimes it can actually save your friendship. So talk things out, give them a second chance, and if it doesn't work, forgive them and move on. You deserve amazing friends! And your ex-friends deserve answers and a chance to move on too. Treat people with respect and kindness. To apply the golden rule to this: break up with your friend how you would want someone to break up with you. Then use your time to invest in building healthy, vibrant, nontoxic relationships. Those are the ones you want to be giving your time and energy to.

FUN THINGS TO DO WITH YOUR FRIENDS

Now let's focus on one of the best parts of friendship: having fun with your friends! It doesn't have to be fancy or glamorous or wildly exciting; having fun can be simple—even if there is absolutely "nothing to do" where you live. You can make your own fun! All you need is a friend, some down time, and some creativity to get started.

The thing is, it's not what you're doing; it's who you're with. That's not to say you don't need to do anything fun with your friends; it's more that you can do pretty much anything with a fun friend and it'll be a good time. Here are some things I like to do with my friends:

- run random errands
- drive down country roads and tell my friend to lean out the window and scream

- make food
- walk around my neighborhood discussing the meaning of life
- go to karaoke and listen to sixty-year-old men attempt to cover CeeLo about ten bpm too slow

You don't want your go-to gals to be people who always expect a red carpet or some fabulous activity. Keep people around who are content to chill on the couch, talking about life, or chase a chicken down the street!

Dani

Here's something fun to do with friends: leave random notes on strangers' cars. I think Christina started this trend in our family. Basically, you write a note (something that's not creepy or scarring) and leave it on a random person's car in a parking lot. You could do it at a place like a grocery store, where people won't be in there for that long, and then sit where you can see their car and watch them read the note! This might sound a little alarming, but it's honestly really entertaining! Just make sure you're not creeping anyone out; write a nice note, like a positive or motivational quote.

Another thing Christina made up is driving to a really good friend's house along with a couple other friends, and then blasting music right outside their house and dancing in the middle of the street. Next, you send them a Snapchat video of you dancing outside of their house, and if they get it fast enough, they'll come out and see you. Or they'll get it later and be really confused as to why you were there . . . (This isn't something you'd do to someone you're not really close to, of course.)

Or have a dance party! Go in your garage, your room—really, anywhere—and blast music. You'll definitely get some hilarious videos out of it.

Katherine

Ideas of what's fun vary from person to person. Some people are much more chill, and they like to just hang out and do relaxing activities together, such as baking or watching a movie. Some people (like me!) are all about the talking and connection, and all they need is a comfy place to talk for hours. Some people really like to go on spontaneous adventures. It's all about knowing yourself and your friends!

Here are some of my ideas:

Keep a journal together where you write each other letters, and pass it back and forth. I did this with one of my best friends, and it was so much fun! This is especially great if you live far apart from each other.

Explore your town together. Find a pretty neighborhood and walk and talk. It's so nice to get some fresh air and exercise while you catch up. Bonus if there's a cool park you can walk to and swing. One of my best friends and I did this together growing up, and going to that park became one of our favorite memories to look back on.

Do a home spa, and give each other face masks and do nails. Super fun and relaxing!

Here are some of our favorite homemade recipes for an at-home spa experience with your friends:

Sugar Scrub

Mix together equal parts coconut oil and sugar, or honey and sugar. This will exfoliate your skin and also provide amazing nutritional benefits.

Oatmeal Honey Face Mask

This is Kath's personal fave. Just mix plain oats (like you'd use to make oatmeal) and honey together in a bowl, apply to your face, and let it soak in for a few minutes. Honey and oats are both soothing to the skin, so this is especially good for red, irritated, or inflamed skin.

Having a spa night with friends is one of our favorite ways to spend an evening. You can invite one or several friends over, or even do it with your siblings. Just make sure you have face masks, candles, calming music, and nail polish to make it a fun experience. If you really want to go all out, fill plastic tubs or large bowls with warm water and Epsom salts, and soak your feet before applying body butter. Relaxing!

Whatever you choose to do with your friends, enjoy your time together, and make lots of memories. Have some adventures. As life goes on, you may have to move away from each other, so enjoy the time you have together while you can! It's so much fun to get to know all the quirks, likes, dislikes, and amazing gifts of the girls in your life. Those friendships could last for ages and bring so much joy to both your lives.

JOURNAL

- What kinds of qualities in a person might be hurtful or toxic, making them not a great candidate for friendship? And what qualities make a good friend?
- What kinds of things can you do to put yourself out there more and get closer with the kinds of girls you need in your life?
- When it comes to being a great friend and keeping your friendships healthy, what are your top two areas you feel you need to work on? What are five actions you can take to start being a better friend in these ways?

PRAY

God, thank You for giving us the gift of friendship. Show us how to be wise and intentional in making and keeping good friends, and reveal to us any unhealthy patterns in our friendships. We want to enjoy life with the friends You have for us!

CHAPTER 4
DATING

EACH OF US SPENT A lot of energy in our teens wondering what in the ever-loving world was going on with the boys around us. Did they like us? Would they ever notice us? Were we doomed to feel insecurity and confusion about boys *forever*? If you're feeling frustrated, know that we all go through it. As crazy as it sounds, relationships with guys and dating can be positive things in your life! If you choose to date (and you don't have to!), it can be a truly worthwhile growing experience, even if you eventually say goodbye to each other.

In this chapter, we want to help you avoid the pitfalls and embrace the positives about dating—but foremost, we want you to know your worth, protect your heart, and use your time wisely.

Lisa

As a young girl just starting to dip your toe into the dating pool, it can be overwhelming trying to figure out what's healthy or okay in relationships. It's easy to think this one magical unicorn person is gonna swoop in and take all your problems away, because that's how it's usually portrayed. The movie starts with a lonely girl who just can't seem to find happiness until—*boom*—she meets a handsome man and "falls in love" in a week's time, and now they're engaged. Wow! His family is rich too?! Oh, he's a prince from a made-up country—duh! Time to honeymoon on a yacht!

You catch my drift. It's unrealistic. So we want to debunk some of the myths you may have learned and give you a clearer view of the other half of the human species.

Remember—guys aren't:

- the deciders for whether we're likable, beautiful, or worthy of love
- the magic solution for making us feel wanted or loved
- fairy-tale princes who will magically fix everything in our lives if we can just find the perfect one
- frightening/scary/to be avoided altogether

Guys are:

- only human, like us: flawed but hilarious and amazing
- also working through challenges and tough times just like we are (teenage years are hard on them too!)
- individuals—we don't need to stereotype them or put them all in one box
- really good friends, brothers, partners, and teammates in life when we get to know and love them in a healthy way

WHAT TO LOOK FOR IN A GUY

When we talk about what to look for in a guy, we're not talking about a long list of traits for the perfect fantasy boyfriend. Dating isn't a fairy tale, and you aren't gonna find a perfect Prince Charming. These are real qualities in real good guys—things we've come to look for and appreciate. We know *we* aren't perfect, and we don't expect perfection in guys either. But knowing what's important to you can steer you where you want to go, and away from where you don't.

Lauren

Everyone has different personality preferences for guys. Some girls like shy guys; some like outgoing guys. Some like artistic ones; some like intellectual ones. And sometimes this changes over time. While everyone is going be drawn to different personality types and even specific physical features, there are a lot of things that you should look for no matter what your type is.

INTEGRITY

Look for a guy who has strong values and beliefs. Someone who strives to do the right thing. Someone you can count on.

SIMILAR VALUES

While it's true that opposites attract, if you're not on the same page about big things, such as morals, religion, political views, or views on life in general, it will be hard to have any kind of a deep relationship. You want to be a team.

EMOTIONAL UNDERSTANDING

Some guys do not know how to deal with feelings at all, so they have no idea how to understand yours. Look for someone who knows how he feels, knows how to express that, and knows how important your feelings are. You want someone to regularly ask how you feel and be willing to listen and help when you need it.

HONESTY

This is so important. Look for someone who can be completely HONEST with you. Someone who will tell you if he is mad at you. If he's hurt by you, he will say it. If he is confused about anything, he will want to clear it up. If he is busy, he will just tell you he's busy and not pretend he might be able to hang out when he knows he can't. If he likes you, he'll tell you—and if he doesn't have feelings for you anymore, he will explain himself to you in a gentle, loving way.

> *Look for someone who can be completely HONEST with you.*

Katherine

To that list I would add:

CHARACTER

His character is what makes him who he is. How does he treat others? What is he living for that is greater than himself? Does he struggle with addiction? Is he honest, or is he always caught up in lies? Does he treat you with respect and make you feel like a queen, or is he disrespectful and dismissive? If you can, pay attention to how he treats his mom and his sisters. This is how he will eventually treat you.

INTEREST

This may seem obvious, but I've known a lot of girls (and been one of those girls) who tend to run after guys who aren't really that interested in them. In my experience, this just makes you feel insecure and embarrassed. It's worth it to be lonely sometimes to wait for someone who really puts in the effort to pursue you.

It's worth it to be lonely sometimes to wait for someone who really puts in the effort to pursue you.

A WARM HEART

This one is big for me. Because of my history of going for guys who were cold and closed off, I've made it a priority to look out for someone who is warm and kind. You will see this in how he treats others. Does he have a natural, genuine smile, speak with kind words, and give gracious compliments to people? Does he go above and beyond as a friend to be considerate and loving to others? Look for the guy who loves to help out and serve.

A STRONG FAITH

I know that if I become the center of a guy's world, it's only a matter of time before the relationship falls apart. Because I am an imperfect and flawed human, I can never satisfy all of another person's needs and desires. But if the love of God—the love that is warm, kind, forgiving, compassionate, and lasts forever—is at the center, this relationship will be strong and beautiful.

Love is patient, love is kind and is not jealous; love does not brag and is not arrogant, does not act unbecomingly; it does not seek its own, is not provoked, does not take into account a wrong suffered, does not rejoice in unrighteousness, but rejoices with the truth; bears all things, believes all things, hopes all things, endures all things.

1 Corinthians 13:4–7

Take a look at this verse from 1 Corinthians. Does the guy you have in mind sound like this? You can even substitute his name to see: for example, "Ryan is patient, Ryan is kind . . ."

Lisa

Picturing myself married to someone can snap me out of a dumb situation *real* fast. If he's not texting you back now, just imagine how bleak things would be fifteen years from now—ha!

> Don't listen to the people telling you to "let loose while you still can," because that's setting you up to form immature habits.

Remember: now is the time to make smart choices and form good habits. Don't listen to the people telling you to "let loose while you still can," because that's setting you up to form immature habits. Your future is not a prison! Start thinking of your future marriage (if that's what you're called to) as a happy, fun, awesome place, and start looking for someone who will help you accomplish that.

Amy

What I look for in a guy has changed *a lot* over time. You will hear many girls saying they want someone funny and charming who

70

drives a Ferrari and also can cook and is secretly Superman. I used to ask for perfection, when I am far from it.

Now I look for a kindhearted, warm guy who knows what he wants (ME! LOL). I also love a man in work boots (I faint), and a man in a truck (I die). I also like guys who are sweet and more introverted. I am a sucker for a handyman too. Can't help it! But most important, I think it's key to look for a confident and kind man who is looking for someone just like you.

GUYS TO AVOID

While we don't want to stereotype or oversimplify guys, we have definitely noticed certain patterns taking place over and over again when it comes to red flags. Guys are only human, and they're going through things just like us. But with many of these "types," leaving them alone will save you heartache.

Christina

THE OVERLY CHARMING GUY WHO SAYS ALL THE PERFECT THINGS

You're probably wondering why this is a bad thing. How could a guy being sweet and nice and saying every little thing you want to hear possibly be a warning sign? They are likely saying all the right things *because they talk to a million girls all the time and have learned all the most effective things to say.*

This guy is *so* good at complimenting, and you are loving it. A lot of girls like him, and you can't believe you "won" the guy lottery. Only, you're not the only winner. Take a step back and realize that if

> *Boys who are sometimes awkward and quirky and give sweet compliments that aren't over-the-top are where it's at.*

a guy has incredible game, it's because he's been playing way, way too much.

My prediction is that soon enough, he's walking away for someone new or you're becoming aware of how many other girls are also "the most beautiful girl" he's ever seen. Think about this: he doesn't even know you yet. So how can he know how great you are? Boys who are sometimes awkward and quirky and give sweet compliments that aren't over-the-top are where it's at. Someone who is "perfect" isn't anywhere near as perfect as he appears.

Dani

THE ELUSIVE, NOCTURNAL, HUMAN-TURNED-HORMONE (ENHTH)

This guy is 100 percent gross. We all know one; he's the boy who creeps up after midnight and sends you the oh-so-infamous late-night texts. Pay attention to the signals your brain sends you to ABORT MISSION when you get a message from this hormone disguised as a beautiful teenage boy.

We all say we aren't gonna fall for his tricks. Every girl laughs it off and pretends that she doesn't care, but deep down, these boys get to us all. At one point or another, we've felt special, even flattered, by the guy who asks us to "hang out" even though we *know* he isn't just looking to talk.

Stay *far* away. This boy will use you and then forget you exist until he gets bored and needs a girl to make him feel good about himself by responding to his desperate beckoning via late-night text.

The danger is multiplied when you actually feel something toward this foul beast of the night.

But don't fret—there is hope for your poor soul. Use the daylight hours to regain your strength, choose the words to reject his late-night texts, and *fight back* for the sake of girls around the world who are falling for him.

THE BOY "NO GIRLS LIKE"

This boy wanders around, whining all day about how many girls reject him. This is offensive to you, because you have a crush on him. He is good-looking and has a good personality, but he just can't accept the fact that someone actually likes him.

This boy was probably rejected badly years back, maybe even a few times, and has grown comfortable being alone. He doesn't *want* to be alone; he is just too scared to get close again after the rejection he experienced.

This guy keeps his distance from the female race by chasing girls who don't like him, getting rejected, and then purposely ignoring the girls who express interest in him because he wants to be the one to reject them for once.

I know one of these. I even used to have a crush on him, and let me tell you: the number of girls who pass him by because he friend-zoned himself is actually appalling. If you show even a hint of feelings toward this creature, he will spontaneously combust and relentlessly friend-zone you. Let him get himself together, and go live your life.

THE GUY WITH IN-PERSON AMNESIA

Have you ever met a guy who texted you every day, but when you ran into him in person, he acted like you didn't exist? You might've told yourself that he was shy, or nervous, or too busy to say

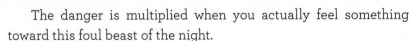

hi, but no. This boy probably has plenty of time and social skills; he's just too lazy to use them on you.

These boys engage in conversation IRL only when you're the last "interesting" person to talk to. If *anyone* he deems cooler than you is around, he will flat-out ignore you. He doesn't want to be your friend—he just wants someone to text. He wants your occasional compliments, your interest in what he's saying, and the feeling of somebody being there for him when he is bored in between classes.

Boys who strictly exist in the cyber world are not to be tolerated.

These boys who strictly exist in the cyber world are not to be tolerated. When it's 3:05 a.m. and they're home alone and dying to send somebody the meme they found on the internet, *don't let that person be you.*

Katherine

THE ICE CUBE

Story of my *life*. I've encountered this boy so many times I could write a book on him. Cold boys—that was my type in my teens. I went for those boys who were mysterious, hard to reach, complex, troubled, emotionally icy, and very critical. And I always, always ended up with frostbite. Ouch.

If you like a boy who is an Ice Cube, he'll start out by showing you his good side.

In the beginning, if he gives you attention, you will feel flattered. *Wow… This is the boy* no girl *can get. And he seems interested in me? I must be so special!* It will be exciting and intoxicating. If he

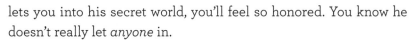

lets you into his secret world, you'll feel so honored. You know he doesn't really let *anyone* in.

But then he reaches his limit. You will soon feel the change; he'll stop texting you as much, and when he does text you, he'll be distant and uninterested. Where he first came on so strong, he will now treat you like you are a nuisance, a burden. You're just like any other person to him—another person who disappointed him by being anything less than superhuman. This will leave you feeling confused, insecure, upset, and frustrated.

The truth is, this boy isn't ready for love. He doesn't know what love is. Maybe one day he will learn, but that day is not today, and you are not the girl to teach him, as bad as you wish you were. Usually he was hurt *really* bad by someone he looked up to when he was younger, and he decided that because that one important person hurt him, *no one* can be trusted, so he doesn't trust anyone. His pain is understandable, but you don't have to put up with his behavior.

If you like someone like this, or you are trying to get over him, I am so, so sorry. This boy's coldness has nothing to do with you. Please get far away from him so you don't become his emotional scratching post. You're worth *sooo* much more.

Lauren

THE TAKEN MAN

This boy has a girlfriend, but he talks to you a lot. You are secretly in love with him, and you know he kind of has a thing for you too. Of course, you're not a home-wrecker, so you don't necessarily flirt with him, but there are some definite vibes when you guys talk. All I can say is *you need to run!* Make no mistake: his girlfriend will always come first. You will always be the second choice! You have probably cried many times over him and wondered, *Why can't he see that I am everything he needs, not some annoying chick?* Yeah, it stinks. And it will always stink. If he wants to keep stringing you along while also being in a relationship with someone else, you have to let him go.

Not to mention, it's not okay to come between two other people—even if you think their relationship is horrible. He needs to realize that for himself. Also keep in mind that if he is talking to you so much when he has a girlfriend, then if you were his girlfriend, he would be doing the same thing with someone else. He feels like he needs to have two girls, but he can't handle just having one. You are not the exception to this. Sorry! Just cut it off now. You might as well do the right thing if you're gonna be hurt either way.

THE MOOD RING

This boy has a mysterious confidence about him. He doesn't really show emotion, and he doesn't really say too much. You can tell there's a lot under the surface, and you want to figure out what he's really like. He doesn't seem to have any major red flags . . . but beware! He will bring you down!

Trying to get close to this guy will seem like a battle. You will be confused because you'll think, *He is a good guy . . . Why am I always so upset about him?* Or, *I just need to get to know him,* but that's the thing. You will never get to know him, because he will never let you! He will constantly push you away with his moodiness. He might be really personable and super close with his guy friends, but with you, he will always make sure he is a mile away.

You know you're with a Mood Ring when you are anxious

every time you see him because you don't know if he's gonna ignore you or be nice today. If this is you, let him know about all the things he does to push you away and how you want to actually be close. If he denies it or gets mad, that's on him. Let him go, and maybe he'll grow from it.

Amy

THE FRIENDLY FLIRT

This guy likes to make you feel special. He will text you with emojis. He will try to single you out. He will hug you tighter than is socially acceptable. He will call you, and you will answer. But this will all be under the guise of "just friends." You may think, *I can be his friend for now. One day he will realize how much he likes me.*

NO, HE WON'T. He likes to have you like him. He likes to feel you care. He likes to have you waiting in the corner. He likes to make you sad about him. *Be warned.* This guy will reel you in until you get yourself off of his hook. It's better to cut your losses and let him go lead another girl on.

The moment you start to move on, *he will text you.* You just have to stay strong. Set yourself free from him.

THE GUY WHO DOESN'T LIKE YOU

If a guy isn't getting your number and texting you and calling you to ask you out, *he doesn't wanna go out with you.* And that is okay. You two just aren't a good match, and that is not your fault. You have to cut your losses and move on. You deserve a

You deserve a guy who will take you out and treat you like a princess.

guy who will take you out and treat you like a princess. If your heart is occupied by a guy who isn't doing a gosh-dang thing, you will miss out on the awesome guy who will. You deserve the sun and moon and stars. Let a guy give that to you.

TEXTING AND GUYS

If you've ever been confused by the cryptic world of texting with guys, you are not alone. How do we handle this strange and confusing form of communication?

Amy

First off, I think texting is lame. It's confusing. It's boring. And it is no substitute for human contact. But if you must text, here is my advice: if he wants to text you, *he will*. You are not gonna lose anything by letting go of a guy who isn't putting in any effort. You are just opening up space for someone who will.

Dani

On the other hand, texting can be a great thing too. It opens doors, breaks ice, and is the battleground for teenage relationships. It can turn tragic, however, if you use it wrong. Here are the most important lessons I've learned about texting boys.

- *Don't always be the first to text.* Especially if you like this guy and want him to like you back. The occasional first text is okay if you've been talking for a while, but I've found that if a guy is interested, he will go to the ends of the earth to find a way to get in your line of communication. If his phone is broken, he'll find a computer. If his mom took it away, he'll steal it back. If nobody paid the phone bill and he can't text, he'll find a friend with a working cell phone. So let it happen naturally.

- *Don't keep texting after you haven't had an answer.* Repeat texting automatically puts you in the desperate zone; and trust me, you do not want to be there. If someone doesn't respond to your text, don't keep trying to get him to talk to you. Remember that if he wants to talk, he will. And take note of minimal effort on his part.

- *Don't let texting be your only form of communication.* It's not an accurate representation of us as people, and honestly, texting gets boring really fast. Try video chatting, or a phone call, or better yet—hang out with the guy in person! Is a relationship that solely exists through a screen really even a relationship?

- *Set limits on yourself.* For one, never *ever* admit feelings for someone by text. You can avoid this by keeping a general rule of not texting boys after 11 p.m. Better yet, 10 p.m. Late at night is when you are tired, not thinking straight, and often feeling vulnerable, and stupid things seem like good ideas. If you're too scared to say it in person, is it really a good idea to say it at all?

FIRST-DATE ADVICE

So you've made a connection with a good guy. You're ready to spend some quality time together to see where it goes. How do you handle a first date?

Lisa

First dates don't have to be awkward, but they usually are—at least a little. Get that out of the way and you'll be fine. Try not to go into it with crazy expectations, and don't go into it trying to win him over. Yes, you should put your best foot forward, but don't think of yourself as some lowly worm who has to fight for his attention and desperately plead for a man to love her. Remember: *you* are the last pickle at the picnic. *You* are the prize. *You* deserve to be wowed too. My advice is to try your best to give him a chance, keep your ears open, keep your eyes peeled for red flags as the conversation goes by, and have faith that it'll work out how it's supposed to.

Remember: you are the last pickle at the picnic. You are the prize.

 FIRST-DATE IDEAS

Meeting for coffee might be the very best first date! You are (a) in a public setting, for safety, and (b) coffee isn't expected to be a long thing, so if it isn't going well, you only have to stick it out for, like, forty-five minutes. It's a very chill environment where you can relax and focus on being yourself. If you're looking for other creative things to do, here are our top picks:

- Go on a bike ride
- Go for a walk
- Take a trip to the park
- See live music or a concert together

- If you live in a city with those rental scooters, go find some and ride around the city
- Try an escape room
- Drive go-carts
- Go bowling
- Get ice cream
- Get breakfast
- Hike, or do something else active/outside

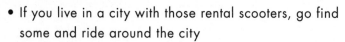

Katherine

I have been on a lot of first dates. It's such an exciting and nerve-racking experience! Here are my best tips for you.

PREPARE

In the few days leading up to your date, do what you need to do to feel good about yourself, nurture yourself, and reflect so when you go on your date you'll be as calm, levelheaded, and relaxed as possible. The morning of the date, I'll pray and ask God to help me be my best self with this person. My go-to prayer: *"If this relationship is meant to be, please help it come together in a beautiful way. If not, please let it fall apart gently."*

WHAT TO WEAR?!

Wear what *you* like, not what you think your date will like on you. It's about being yourself, not pleasing him! After all, it's a first date. You still need to figure out if you like him.

Make sure to wear something that goes with whatever you're doing. If it's a restaurant, find out if it's fancy or more casual. If it's an active date, make sure you have good shoes for it! Overall, wear something that makes you feel comfortable, and be yourself. I like

Wear what you like, not what you think your date will like on you.

to be modest in general because I feel more comfortable that way. When I'm not constantly tugging on a shirt that's falling down or a skirt that's riding up, I feel like I can relax and be myself.

MAKEUP

I like to wear natural, simple makeup, so my date can look at my face and not be distracted by any bright colors or a lot of dark eye makeup. But then again, that's just my style. If makeup is your thing and you like to be creative, I say go for it! Be yourself.

Lauren

Going into the date, instead of thinking, *Does he like me?* think, *Do I like him?* Don't get caught up in getting him to like you. Ask him real questions about who he is and get to know what his opinions are on things that are important to you. Figure out what he stands for, what he thinks is important in life.

Don't put too much pressure on it! It's just one date. You do not owe the guy anything, and you never have to talk to him ever again if you don't want to.

If you don't actually like him, don't lead him on and act like you like him. You can let him down gently if he asks you out again.

Going into the date, instead of thinking, Does he like me? think, Do I like him?

But if this is a nice, good person who seems stable and caring, consider *giving him another chance.* Just because you don't feel sparks flying yet doesn't mean you won't in the future.

Amy

This sounds cliché, but just be yourself. Show your date your personality. You won't know if your personalities are a good match if you're not being your true self with him. That's what dating is about. It's all about getting to know people and which personality types and qualities fit with you. You are the one deciding if you want

It's not anyone's fault, and there is nothing wrong with you if your personalities don't fit.

to date a guy, and sometimes people just aren't a good match. It's not anyone's fault, and there is nothing wrong with you if your personalities don't fit.

Katherine

When I was a teenager, I had it in my head that boys only liked Christina and Lisa, and not me. I felt invisible to boys. It was so frustrating. I thought that boys only liked girls who were sassy and teased them a lot. But that wasn't my personality. I didn't feel comfortable being super sassy. I like to be playful when I know someone well, but being sassy right from the start is not my style.

It took me a long time to realize that I am Katherine—more on the sweet side, goofy, quirky, nurturing, soft, sensitive, deep, spiritual, adventurous, a dreamer. I realized I didn't have to change. If I loved who I truly am, the right kinds of guys would see that and be drawn to it. It's so much better that way, because there is no better feeling than when someone sees you for who you truly are and *loves* it. It's a very healing experience.

BREAKING UP

Not every dating relationship is meant to last forever. How do we know when it's time to let go? And how do we start that difficult conversation?

Relationships are hard, and they definitely require work, but a relationship should not be *all* work! You want to feel safe, respected, comfortable, and happy in your relationship. If you don't, something needs to change. If someone is making you feel insecure, uncomfortable, unsafe, or if he seems to be making your life worse, that is *not good*. Get out of there! You shouldn't be putting all your time and energy into someone who is doing that.

Relationships are hard, and they definitely require work, but a relationship should not be all work!

On the other hand, if you find yourself in a relationship where you really care about the person, but you're not sure if it's right anymore, these are some things to think about:

- Does he make me feel valued and important?
- Do I feel like I can be myself around him?
- Does he support my goals and help me reach them?
- Is he honest with me when he's upset?
- When I am honest with him about my feelings, does he respect and value them?
- Do I feel relaxed when I am with him, before I see him, and after I see him?

Basically, you need to ask yourself if he is adding to your life or subtracting from it. And if he is subtracting from it, are these things you can talk to him about and try to fix, or are they just a part of who he is? I think you should always at least try to fix things before you decide to end the relationship. But if you have told him about things that he's doing that need to change and he doesn't change them, you have to accept that and let him go.

Lauren

The most important thing in a breakup conversation is to *be honest*. If the guy has real problems that are ruining the relationship, *he needs to know*. He might ruin future relationships if no one ever tells him what he's doing wrong. Also, I know from experience that there is nothing worse than someone either randomly disappearing from your life without telling you why, or ending things without giving you a reason.

Be respectful. Don't call him names or be rude about his short-comings. Even if he did something really bad, it's better to keep the conversation about how his actions made you feel and why it wasn't okay; don't resort to name-calling and yelling.

Be firm. If you know you want a relationship to be over and that it's not good for you, don't let him push you into prolonging it, even if he says, "I will change!" or "Just give me time!" You've made up your mind. If you don't want to be with him, that's not gonna change no matter what he says.

HOW TO GET OVER SOMEONE

A broken heart can make you feel like you are literally dying. Whether you've broken up with someone or he's broken up with you, it's going to *hurt*. But whether he let you down easy or completely shattered your heart with an out-of-the-blue breakup, you can pick yourself up again and take steps to heal. Here's how to begin.

> He heals the brokenhearted and binds up their wounds.
> PSALM 147:3

Let yourself be sad about the breakup. Let yourself be mad about it. Let yourself be happy about it. Whatever you feel about it, let yourself feel it—because even if you think you have no feelings about it, you *definitely* do. If you are really upset about it or mad or disappointed, *that's okay*. You have these feelings for a reason, and if you ignore them, they will not go away. If you ever want to move on, you have to express them. Here are some ways you can express your feelings:

- Go on a long walk and listen to songs that describe how you feel about the breakup.
- Get a notebook and dedicate it solely to writing about how you feel about the situation.
- Talk to your friends about it. Tell them, "Hey, look: I really need to talk about this, and I just need you to listen." Tell them the whole story, even if they already know it, and everything you think and feel about it.
- Put away everything that reminds you of your ex-boyfriend, and let go of the past. Do a full-on cleanse, and think of the future.

Dani

This section is not for advice on how to get over a guy who's great and you're still good friends with. This is for people who need to get over the kind of guy who ruins lives and creates rivers of tears.

The first step to getting over an ex like this is cutting *all* ties. This sounds extreme, but if you're heartbroken, you have to take extreme measures to move on. Delete, unfollow, block, whatever you have to do to make sure you never see *anything* he posts on social media.

Also, do not stalk him. Don't ask other people how he's doing. You don't need to know if he's found someone else. Get involved in your *own* life instead of trying to keep up with your ex's, through social media or otherwise.

Remember: you must express your feelings if you want to move on. During the day, you can feel free to be fun and carefree and excited 'cause you're newly single and—whoo!—life is great. But at night, it is *on*. Cry your eyes out, write dramatic letters to your ex (never share these, *ever*), and be super expressive. *Overly* expressive.

The best way to get over someone and get him out of your head is to keep his name out of your mouth! When you put a stop to all contact, that is when the real moving on happens.

> The best way to get over someone and get him out of your head is to keep his name out of your mouth!

But it only happens when you want it to. You only move on if you genuinely want to. If you don't yet want to, find the reason to, because I promise you—it's there.

SETTING BOUNDARIES

Katherine

Setting physical boundaries in dating is an incredibly personal, sticky subject. Many people feel a lot of shame even just thinking about it. I was hesitant to write this section because I know how touchy it is, but I thought that it might be beneficial to simply share my personal story and my thoughts on it.

Growing up as a teenager in the mid-2000s, my main lessons in dating came from *Seventeen* magazine and reality TV shows. The message I got was, "Do whatever you want with your body!" While it is true that we can make our own choices, no one talked about how serious it is to hook up or have sex and how vulnerable and life-changing it is. In middle school I started hearing stories with graphic details about who had hooked up with who, who was "a thing," and who was dating . . . until they broke up two weeks later.

Whenever anyone talked about who had done what with whom, they always had these mischievous, scandalous expressions on their faces. The way they talked about it made it seem dirty and bad. I didn't really understand what all of it meant, so I decided to stay far away. I held hands with a few guys in early high school, but that was pretty much it.

Until I met . . . him. I was seventeen, and he was the first boy I ever really fell for. He had a reputation for partying, hooking up with a lot of girls, and generally being a "bad boy." I was completely the opposite. I had already decided I was never going to drink, I never went to parties, and I had zero experience with guys physically. He and I started hanging out all the time, and I was obsessed with him. I thought about him constantly and wondered when I was going to see him next.

Miraculously, during the exact time that I was meeting up with him to hang out one-on-one at night (usually at a park by my house), my mom started giving me books on purity, which is a Christian term meaning to live out your sexuality in a way that honors God. One of the books mentioned saving your first kiss for your wedding day, and it immediately struck me as something I wanted to do. One night I was praying, and I felt as though God was confirming to me that, yes, this was something I was meant to do.

I told this boy that I wanted to save my first kiss for my wedding day, and he laughed. He said he would "hire" one of his friends to come up and kiss me when I wasn't expecting it. Ew.

Pretty soon after that, I broke things off with him, and I'm thankful to say my first kiss wasn't wasted on him or someone he hired!

To whoever is reading this right now, I want to say, first of all, you are so loved and valuable no matter what you have or have not done sexually. I also want to be clear: I don't think kissing before your wedding is bad or sinful at all! It's just something I made a personal choice to do, and I'm very happy I did. I'm twenty-seven now and engaged, and I am so, so glad I made that decision ten years ago. Although it's been hard and sometimes lonely, and there were times I almost broke that promise to myself, I believe it saved me a lot of heartache and confusion.

I can only speak from my own experience, but I want to say that if you are thinking of saving yourself for marriage, or even saving your first

I told this boy that I wanted to save my first kiss for my wedding day, and he laughed.

kiss like me, I encourage you with all of my heart to do so. It's a very personal decision, and I think it's something you have to have a very strong reason for (like a promise to God and to yourself). Otherwise it's not going to happen. Also, I suggest doing some research—something that has really helped me develop physical boundaries. I read several books, including *If You Really Loved Me* by Jason Evert, *How to Find Your Soulmate Without Losing Your Soul* by Jason and Crystalina Evert, and *Captivating* by John and Stasi Eldredge, as well as studied St. John Paul II's incredible work called *Theology of the Body*. Those books were so important to me when I was making my decision.

Your physical boundaries are your choice, not the guy's you are dating. It's so important for us girls to speak up and be extremely clear about what we will and will not do in dating as early as possible. Before I met my fiancé, I used to tell guys within the first couple of dates, "I am saving myself for marriage, and I am also saving my first kiss for my wedding day." You could also use clear language like, "I am saving sex for marriage and that also includes anything below the belt. I am okay with kissing and holding hands, but that's all. I don't want to go any further." I know that might feel awkward or blunt, but your body is so precious and worth it. You have to stand up for yourself, and let me be clear—you do not owe a guy anything. If he buys you dinner, you say, "Thank you for dinner." Do you owe him a kiss? Or even a handshake? Nope. Nothing.

Last, I want to say, if you have made choices with your boundaries that you regret, it is never too late to start fresh. You can choose any day to save yourself for marriage from now on. I have close friends who lost their virginity before marriage and then decided to wait from a certain point on, and they have said they were so happy they chose to wait with the person they ended up marrying, even though that wasn't the case originally.

Plus, there are a lot of unexpected benefits to setting boundaries from the beginning.
The less of a physical element your relationship has, the less complicated it will be, and
the more clear-headed you will be to discern
if this is the right person for you. (Look up
the science of sex—all the intense hormones it
releases make our minds very clouded when
making decisions.) Yes, you have the choice to save as much or as
little as you want for marriage, but I recommend looking into it and
doing the research before you make that choice. I really do believe,
after doing my own research, that God created sex to be within
marriage—and if you follow that plan He made, you will have a lot
more true happiness and peace of mind in relationships. And I say
that from my own experience!

> Do you not know that your body is a temple of the Holy
> Spirit who is in you, whom you have from God, and that you
> are not your own? For you have been bought with a price:
> therefore glorify God in your body.
>
> 1 CORINTHIANS 6:19–20

Christina

When it came to physical boundaries in dating, this was something
I'd thought through very thoroughly. Before I got into seriously dating boys, I didn't have much in mind when it came to standards. As
sad as that is, it's true. But as I got into the dating world, it quickly
became apparent to me that there were a lot of guys out there who
wanted to know exactly what my boundaries or standards were (if
I even had any), and they wanted to know for different reasons.

Some, so they could respect my boundaries. Others, so they could see how far they could push them. And others so that they could see if they even wanted to get involved with me at all. And that third reason particularly is what makes me so passionate about this topic.

When I realized that there were certain guys who would completely lose interest in a girl when they realized they wouldn't get what they wanted physically out of her—and therefore, she wasn't worth dating at all—it made me realize two things. First, that I needed to avoid those guys. Second, that I could learn a lot about a guy by telling him my boundaries.

I made the decision to save myself for marriage at around age sixteen or seventeen. I was NOT always planning on this, but the more I researched it, the more I wanted to make the decision I did. Speaking from my personal experience of waiting till marriage, I believe that when it comes to specific boundaries, this can vary from person to person based on how different physical actions affect them. For instance, some people can have kissing as a part of their relationship, whereas for others, kissing someone can be too much and tempt them to want to go further. You have to know yourself and what actions will express genuine affection versus lead you down the wrong path. For me, it all came down to asking myself one question: What is the end goal here? Mine was to find the man who would stand by me for the rest of my life—my life partner. My teammate who'd be by my side through thick and thin, who I could trust with anything and everything, and who would love me at my worst and most vulnerable. The man who

I can learn a lot about a guy by telling him my boundaries.

would see the darkest and weakest parts of me and still choose me every day, regardless of how he felt about me at that particular moment.

I made that goal at a young age, and I realized I was embarking on a challenge. I knew that to make such a life-changing and big decision, I had to keep my eyes wide open and be very particular and selective. I did not want to be blindsided and become infatuated or delusional about a guy and think he was so amazing when he was clearly not. This was something I noticed happening around me with my friends, and I even fell into it a few times before I snapped myself out of it. I'd see my friends become obsessed with some guy who was not even treating them well and didn't deserve their constant affection and attention, and I'd wonder what the heck was going on—until I found myself in the same situation. It was then that I realized how much attention and affection from a guy can cloud your judgment! It can feel so good to be liked, touched, or paid attention to by a guy to the point that you basically forget how to think. All you can focus on is how good it feels to get their affection and when you can get it next, and this scared me. I didn't want to be in such an infatuated mind-set when trying to discern whether a guy was actually treating me right and if I should continue dating him or not.

Knowing that and keeping in the back of my mind that what I really wanted at the end of the day was to be truly loved, I decided that I needed to be clear with guys on my physical boundaries right up front so I could eliminate the ones who didn't respect me and find the man who would truly love me. I wanted to be able to focus on getting to know each other deeply and authentically without too much physical affection to get me overly excited and confused when I was trying to make a very important and

Attention and affection from a guy can cloud your judgment!

life-changing decision. However, this didn't mean I decided never to touch the guy I was dating. I love physical affection, and there are so many ways to be caring and loving physically that create connection but don't get me too excited to think straight. Holding hands, hugging and kissing (if that feels right for you) can be great ways of expressing affection without heading down the wrong path. And that's where the "it can vary from person to person" part comes in. Some people need stricter boundaries than others depending on how physical affection affects them. Weigh the pros and cons and consider your end goal, talk to your parents or a trusted adult, realize how important your love life truly is, and make the decision for yourself.

From my personal experience, this was a decision I made first based in logic and reason and then later based on my religious beliefs. It took me some time to learn about the spirituality of it all, but by the time I did, I was hooked. I started studying sex and waiting until marriage from a Christian perspective, and I was shocked by how different it was from what I had learned previously from the world. Before, it had seemed like Christian teaching on sex was just a bunch of rules to follow. I didn't understand why I needed to follow them. But after really looking into it, I discovered that God has a plan for the human body and sexuality. His plan is to give us freedom from the enslavement of lust, which basically means using another person as an object for our own pleasure. I believe we were each made to give ourselves as a total gift to the person we marry. God's plan can sometimes seem mysterious, but He knew what He was doing. I can say now that if I were to go back and do it all over again, I would 100 percent make the same choice to wait until marriage.

I hear the argument a lot that people don't think they'd truly know each other or know if they're compatible if they wait until marriage to get physical, but now that I'm married, I can

I believe we were made to give ourselves as a total gift to the person we marry.

say that it was the deep talks, tough things we went through together, and vulnerable moments of opening up to each other that led us to becoming truly known by each other. I am happy to report from married life that my choice turned out to serve me immensely throughout my dating experience, and it did not hinder the "getting to know each other" process at all from my perspective. On the contrary, I believe it allowed us to get closer because we focused more on exploring each other intellectually, emotionally, and spiritually than physically. I firmly believe that this decision led me down a very good path, and I'm so grateful for teenage Christina doing all of her research and making that decision.

HOW TO ENJOY BEING SINGLE

If you are currently not involved in a relationship, please know that being single can be a powerful, strengthening, and even fun and enjoyable place to be. That's not just something we say to make you feel better. It's the absolute truth. Here are some of our experiences being single.

Being single can be a powerful, strengthening, and even fun and enjoyable place to be.

Katherine

I'm twenty-seven, and up until I was twenty-five, I was pretty much always single. So I know this territory well. Not gonna lie—there are moments where it feels like you're in an echoing cave of loneliness, and you want to scream. There are times when seeing *all* of your close friends get boyfriends and not having one yourself can make you feel worthless and terrified. You may be thinking, *What's wrong with me?* Answer: nothing. You're fine. Deep breath.

I think the best way to enjoy being single is to truly get to know yourself. What are your likes and dislikes? What was something that happened to you that really affected you? What are you secretly hoping for? What makes you smile, no matter how bad your day has been?

Finding out who you are will help you be comfortable with yourself. Being comfortable with yourself helps you fall in love with yourself. And loving who you are is the best way to go about life, whether you're dating someone or not.

Loving who you are is the best way to go about life, whether you're dating someone or not.

So I say, go on a great adventure of self-discovery. Read great books. Listen to hundreds of songs, and develop your unique music taste. Go on walks in nature, and think deep thoughts. Love your family and friends with the best of your heart. Try new things. Volunteer. Grow and grow and never stop growing. You've got *so much* to give.

Amy

I never enjoyed being single . . . until recently. Truly miraculous! I have had a total shift in my mind-set; I once thought a relationship would define and fulfill me. But I realized I am not ever going to find fulfillment in another person, and being single isn't a curse I need to break. It is a beautiful time of exploration and learning about yourself on your own. I am really loving that aspect of the single season of my life now.

Being single is a lot of things. It's fun, it's depressing, it's adventurous, it's empowering, and it can get lonely, especially when you are watching romantic comedies. Being single is the time to spread your wings. Find yourself. People sometimes act like you can just purchase a relationship on Amazon. Two-day delivery, and you are set, like it's something you have any control over. But the more you try to control these things, the more it backfires. This is the time for you to open your heart and figure out what you truly want out of life, and that doesn't have to involve a relationship.

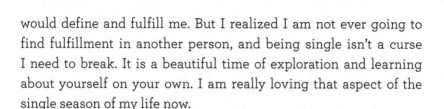

From my experience, loneliness doesn't come from being single; it comes from isolating yourself.

Isolation kills! Don't let it take your life! Make your life a happy place *right now*. Don't wait for a boy; don't wait for college; don't wait for five years from now, when it's all figured out (which it never will be). Just start *now* to make life as enjoyable and meaningful as you can.

Also, let me say that I was approached by the best guy I've ever met at a time in my life when I was genuinely so grateful to be alive, so connected to my family, and for the first time not even thinking about meeting anyone in that way. Good things come when we least expect them. So stop expecting them so hard, and start having fun with what you already have! Believe in yourself first, love and respect yourself first, and you'll be in a good place no matter what happens.

JOURNAL

- What do you think are the most important qualities to look for in a person to date? What red flags have you encountered?
- Do you think you have any expectations about dating that may not be based in reality? What are they?
- What are some mind-sets regarding dating, guys, and singleness that you want to leave behind? What are some you want to cultivate?

PRAY

Lord, please protect my heart and give me grace and perspective as I get to know the boys in my life. Show me how to grow in strength and wisdom in all my relationships—with myself and with the guys You put in my path.

CHAPTER 5

FAMILY

SOMETHING A LOT OF PEOPLE don't know about us is that it's not just us six sisters—we also have five brothers. Growing up homeschooled in a family of eleven kids, we faced a lot of challenges in learning to understand, appreciate, and respect one another and our parents. Because all of us have such different personalities, we needed to develop communication skills and grace for the messiness of our big family. So we went about figuring out how to do it.

The "older generation" of us sisters is incredibly passionate about psychology. For years we would spend hours reading psych books on how to build healthy relationships. We are by no means experts, but we did notice a lot of improvement and change in our family when we started applying some of the principles we'd learned from books—principles about opening up and communication.

At first it felt kind of radical and crazy. As kids, we kept our problems quiet and tried to deal with our heartbreak, failures, and mistakes on our own. This did not work. We bottled up our emotions, and many of us felt isolated, even in a big family like ours. Then one day Christina (naturally, the oldest sister) spoke up and shared her feelings for the first time. What followed was a series of lengthy family talks. Raw honesty, tears, and the release of pent-up emotions felt groundbreaking.

Today our family is so much closer and shares a much stronger, more loving bond. The eleven of us siblings are like a fierce tribe. If someone hurts one of us—you'd better watch out! We are *far* from perfect. Deep issues come up on a regular basis. But the difference is that now we talk about what we are going through. We rally together to support whoever is struggling. The result is imperfect but filled with love.

In this chapter we want to share what we've learned about communicating better with your parents and siblings and how to get closer to your family, as well as ideas for fun activities to do with them. We hope it will inspire you to find moments for family bonding and build stronger relationships with your siblings and parents.

> The eleven of us siblings are like a fierce tribe. If someone hurts one of us—you'd better watch out!

HOW TO GET CLOSER TO YOUR FAMILY

Our family gives us our first view of the world—they're the first people we learn to interact with. They give us our expectations for what love and life will be like. Unfortunately, a lot of us are not as close with our families as we would like to be. It can be hard to open up to our siblings and parents. We think they may make fun of us or that they won't understand. Maybe you told your brother something personal or vulnerable and he made fun of you. Maybe you told your mom something and she brushed it off, or she just didn't understand where you were coming from. Or maybe you and your family members have so much going on that you've forgotten how to be friends in addition to family members. When things like that happen, we often close ourselves off to avoid getting hurt. If you feel closed off from your family, for this reason or any other, we encourage you to start to open up again. Here are our tips on how to start building your relationship with your family.

Amy

Start small. Ask your brother how he is doing, and really mean it. Maybe tell your mom about something that happened at school or in your life this week. Try it with the little stuff first, and work up to the bigger stuff. If family members have hurt you or blown you off in the past, they probably didn't mean to. It's good to tell them if something they said hurt your feelings so they have a chance to explain. Even if they did mean what they said and it was hurtful, at least you have had an honest conversation about it. You might even ask them to apologize if you can tell them in a calm way what they did that hurt you. But even if they don't, try to forgive. Forgiveness is essential in a relationship if you want to be close with someone. Let them into your life, and ask them about theirs. Ask them to hang out or maybe watch a movie with you—simple things that let them know they matter to you. It can be scary to take the initiative; you might be scared of being rejected, but even if they can't hang out that day, you will feel great knowing you put in the effort.

> Forgiveness is essential in a relationship if you want to be close with someone.

Lauren

Maybe you think your siblings or parents are really annoying and dumb—and maybe sometimes they are—but the truth is, they are the people who stay with you forever, through everything, no matter what. If you lose everything or something really bad happens to you, friends are not necessarily going to stick around. But your family will. And if you spend your life ignoring them or being rude to them, you will most definitely regret it! If you want to get closer with your family and you don't know how, the main thing to do is talk to them more. Ask them how their day went; ask them how they're feeling; ask them about something they are really interested in; or suggest doing something with the whole family or with just one family member (more ideas on that later).

You'll never regret trying to work on your relationship with your family.

Even if they are rude or reject you for that, know that they still appreciate you reaching out. It can take time. Ultimately, you can't force anyone to be close with you, but as long as you put in the effort and let your family know you're there for them and that you care about them, that's all that matters. You'll never regret trying to work on your relationship with your family.

Dani

Here's what you have to know about being close with your siblings: most likely your brothers or sisters want to be close with you. We are humans, and we need connection. Your siblings might be mean and act like they don't want to talk to you, but chances are, if you take an interest in their lives, they will let you come closer to them little by little, and your relationship will grow.

How to begin? Try going into their rooms more to talk, or ask them to hang out one night, or just start telling them about your life. Things will grow from there. If you and your siblings aren't close, remember that it's just like a friendship—you can't just dive right into your deep insecurities the first time you really talk, because the trust isn't there. Give it time.

Katherine

I am a highly sensitive person, and it took me a very long time to realize something very important about my siblings: when they are in bad moods, most of the time it has nothing to do with me! I used to get stressed and frustrated when one of them started being moody and immediately I would think, *What did I do wrong?* I always thought it was my fault.

I share this to illustrate something very important I've learned: everyone has a unique personality, and everyone processes things differently. One of the greatest things about having siblings is learning how to handle different personalities.

I encourage you to look for the best in your family members. I know it's easier to see the worst, especially when you're in close quarters with them and they get on your nerves. But everyone has a lot of beauty and goodness in them, and if you open yourself up, you might find yourself appreciating your family more than ever.

BUILDING COMMUNICATION

Once you've opened the door to becoming closer with your family, you'll find you need to communicate. But because old habits die hard, we as humans tend to stick to unhealthy communication habits with family. A lot of times we don't think before we speak to our family members because we're so comfortable. But the power of words will surprise you. Changing the way you talk to your family can seriously change the course of your family's life.

> Pleasing words are a honeycomb, sweet to the taste and invigorating to the bones.
>
> PROVERBS 16:24

> Death and life are in the power of the tongue; those who choose one shall eat its fruit.
>
> PROVERBS 18:21

Lauren

A big problem with family communication is the *lack* of it. For instance, you are mad at your sister 'cause she did something irritating, but instead of saying, "Hey, look. I'm mad at you," you say something rude or make fun of her when you get a chance. This is called being *passive-aggressive*. This is the poison that kills relationships every day. Start being *honest* instead of being passive-aggressive. Tell your siblings and parents when they hurt your feelings, and stop hurting them back on purpose, even if you're mad at them. It doesn't help anything to be rude; it honestly just makes your life worse. You have to live with these people and see them every day; why would you make your living quarters a tense and angry place? Be nice; be kind, *even* when you're mad. Let it go, and be the bigger person—it will only make your life better and easier.

Amy

Do not give your family the silent treatment. It strains your relationships, and there is this underlying tension all the time if you are being passive-aggressive. You have to be firm in your boundaries and express them in healthy ways. You gotta let out your frustration and anger and hurt. Journaling and writing letters help you sort out your feelings before you speak to your family and bring up what is bothering you. I have used this a lot to figure out exactly how I am feeling. I have a tendency to freeze people out or blow up at them when I get upset. I know I have to work on these things, so I have been making my way back to the middle and expressing myself calmly and in healthy ways.

Here are a few examples of unhelpful ways to say things:

- "That harmony you sang sounded like a blaring train horn."
- "You're acting like a psycho!"
- "Maybe if you weren't so disorganized, you could actually get something done."

And here are some helpful ways to say the same things:

- "Sing your harmony more softly so it complements the rest of the group."
- "It's hard to discuss things when you're upset. maybe we should take ten minutes to cool down and then talk about this calmly."
- "Have you tried making a scheduled to-do list and writing down how long each task takes?"

Thinking about helpful versus unhelpful communication has really helped me this year!

Dani

With family, sometimes you think that because you're so close with them (emotionally or even just physically, living in the same house), you can say anything and it won't matter. Believe it or not, your siblings and/or parents have feelings too. It probably sounds ridiculous for me to say that, but it's something a lot of us forget. So sometimes we find ourselves in situations where we're having an issue with a family member and we explode—yelling or calling names or being overly aggressive because we want to tell someone our exact thoughts and express how upset we are—but that honestly just makes things worse. You end up hurting feelings and unintentionally triggering people into defense mode. If you have an issue with a family member, plan what you're going to say. Even if you're emotional in the moment, get out of the situation and write about it. Write down how your family member makes you feel, what you want him or her to do instead, and how you could improve the relationship. *Then* have an honest conversation where you express your feelings and try to fix the issue.

Believe it or not, your siblings and/or parents have feelings too!

> How good and how pleasant it is, when brothers dwell together as one!
>
> PSALM 133:1

Lauren

Something that's really important in family relationships is learning how to support and show up for your family. Everyone feels love and shows love in different ways. Once, I wrote a list of the ways I feel supported and shared it with my sisters. Things like asking me if I need help with anything and then doing something for me, such as vacuuming my car or helping me organize my closet or helping me clean my room. Then all my sisters wrote lists of what makes them feel supported, and we all read them to each other. We realized that the way you show love to someone is not always going to get that across to them, because the way they feel loved is completely different from the way you feel loved. So if you want to feel closer to your family members, try asking them what actually means the most to them!

HOW TO COMMUNICATE
WITH YOUR PARENTS

Communicating with parents can be extra tricky because of the authority they have over us and the massive influence they have on our lives. In the teenage years, we start to see that our parents are just human beings like us, and that means—like us—they are not perfect. Communicating with our parents with compassion, understanding, and a level head can seem completely unrealistic at times, but we promise—it's possible, with a little bit of work.

Katherine

Growing up, it was hard for me to communicate with my mom because I felt like she didn't value what I valued. I am a *very* social person, and I always wanted to be with my friends whenever possible. When I was a teen, my mom and I would argue a lot because it seemed like she was against me seeing my friends. I would ask to go to one of their houses, and she would ask, "Why?" The thing is, my mom is an introvert, so to want to see my friends pretty much at every free moment was a foreign concept to her.

When I got older, I started to realize that she had good intentions. She wanted me to learn my limits and be balanced. When I got my car and moved out, I got in a bad habit of overscheduling myself to the point of exhaustion and even getting sick a lot! I realized that although my mom seemed crazy to me when I was younger, she had some wisdom to share about balancing my schedule, and now I appreciate that.

I encourage you to give your parents a break, because even though they are probably a bit unreasonable at times, they really love you and want what's best for you.

I encourage you to give your parents a break, because even though they are probably a bit unreasonable at times, they really love you and want what's best for you. You have to be your own person and live your life, but also try to listen to what they have to say. They have lived on this earth a lot longer than you have, so their opinion is worth hearing!

Lauren

You may not realize this, but your parents aren't trying to ruin your life. They don't hate you! They actually really want you to talk to them and hang out with them. Maybe they have a tendency to be controlling or don't know how to connect, but the truth remains: most parents really care about you and want you to be close with them. They want you to have a good life. With that said, if you have a problem with them, you need to tell them. If they are making you feel guilty, ashamed, anxious, or upset, tell them! It is your responsibility to yourself to communicate your feelings to them and try to fix anything that's weighing you down or messing with your health and well-being. (Of course if you're actually experiencing abuse, please tell a trusted adult so you can get some help.)

When you talk, avoid "you" statements, such as, "You are so rude!" or "You are ruining my life!" Make "I" statements, such as, "I feel really hurt when you . . ." or "I feel like you don't care about . . ." Yelling, insulting, and attacking don't work. This just puts them on the defensive and doesn't help anything. Your goal should be to express yourself openly and respectfully and come to some sort of conclusion or compromise. You will never regret trying to fix your relationship with your parents, but you will always regret it if you never try.

Dani

You cannot and will not survive living under your parents' roof if you aren't *honest* with them. Tell them if you're mad, if you think they are mistreating you, and also tell them that you appreciate them and love them. Your parents love you, and they want your life to be good. No matter what they say, nine out of ten parents probably do want you to succeed in life, believe it or not.

Your parents are gonna find it really hard to treat you well if you don't treat them well. They love you and they want to be close with you, so *let them*, 'cause they're not gonna be here forever.

Amy

I know I spent many years being angry and huffing around and trying to get my parents to listen and see things my way. It can be kinda awkward when you are becoming an adult and you're still under your parents' roof. The most effective way to get your parents to listen and respect you is to try your best to objectively listen and respect them up front (which I know can be really, really hard). I've had to learn to listen to what my mom and dad have to say and then weigh it against my own sense of reason and my own experience.

Lisa

Let's be real: parents aren't always the easiest people to talk to. It can be tough to get your way, feel heard, or even speak at all sometimes. The best thing to do in tough situations is to prepare ahead of time when you have to talk something over with them. Get yourself in a relaxed state, plan what you wanna ask for, respect them the way you want them to respect you, and then accept whatever happens. In any relationship, communication is key. Talking things out when you're upset, hurt, or need something is so important. I know it's scary to say how you feel sometimes, but just remember that the best way to get over your fears is to face them. Also, remember that people can't read your mind. If you need or want something, you have to say it clearly and let it be known. Don't expect people to know what you want! It's really hard to speak up, but the most rewarding things in life don't come easily. Your parents love you and want you to be happy—so help them help you!

And don't forget: you can have fun with your parents too. My favorite ways to bond with my parents are going on walks together and going out for breakfast. I know what it's like to feel like your parents don't really know you because you keep so much inside, but I encourage you to start small today and have some lighthearted hangs with your parents one-on-one; maybe invite them to watch a movie with you or go

Don't forget: you can have fun with your parents too.

grab coffee together and just talk about fun stuff. It's the first step to building a friendship that can truly change your life!

HOW TO HAVE FUN
WITH YOUR FAMILY

Sometimes the best kind of communication is just to have fun together. Every family is different, but when you grow up, the fun things you do with your family will become some of your most treasured memories. When you find out what kinds of things are fun to do together as a family, you can start building a stronger bond with your fam.

Amy

I know you might be wondering why spending time with your family is important, but when you get to know those who are closest to you on a deep level, it can be so fulfilling.

The best things to do together are active things. Here are some ideas:

- You can play some board games or card games. (Our family once spent seven hours playing the card game Hearts one Easter. And it was amazing!)
- If your family likes sports, play your favorite sport with everyone.
- Movie nights can be really fun. Our family loves to mix popcorn with M&M's for movie nights.
- Try doing fun, holiday-themed stuff during the holiday season. One of our favorite things to do is throw parties with

a bunch of our friends for the different holidays. Because we're all different ages, we have friends of every age group all together!

It's all about trying new things. Your family may not be receptive to every idea you have, but have courage and put yourself out there. Don't be offended if it doesn't work out the first time. Remember that it's all about effort; putting in that effort will show that you care. You will find something that works, so give it a try!

Lauren

Here are some of my top family outing ideas:

- Go bowling
- Go ice skating
- Go to dinner
- Go get ice cream
- Go on a walk or a bike ride
- Go get coffee
- Make dinner together
- Go to the movies or a concert

Dani

Hanging out with your family can be super annoying because, like, friends exist, but it can also be really fun! All thirteen of us hang out together sometimes, and it gets *lit*.

Game nights are a classic family tradition, so try getting your family together to play Monopoly, Apples to Apples, Bowl of Nouns, or any other games that you have.

If you have younger siblings, take them on an adventure. Go on a hike, a walk, or a bike ride, or go swimming, run through the woods, or even make up a game. Spend time outside with little kids and you'll feel really good after. Take advantage of the fact that you're older, and *lead them*.

If you have siblings who are old (over sixteen) and boring, come up with a plan to hang out somewhere, make them teach you how to drive (responsibly), get them to take you to the grocery store, or come up with a really random idea, and you'll find that simple things can be really enjoyable.

We like a game called Flashlight Tag that's really fun to play outside at night.

1. One person is "it," and the rest of the people run and hide.
2. "It" wanders around with a flashlight, looking for the other people.
3. If the light shines on you, you're out! Super fun and kinda scary. Recommended by 10/10.

Get back in touch with your inner child, because the most fun things to do with your family are "childish" things.

Christina

The fun times you have with your family can be some of your very best memories. Instead of taking family time for granted, realize you won't always be able to be together like this. Make a personal commitment to be positive, be in the moment, and try your best to truly cherish time together. I challenge you to have a family fun night at least once a week, even if it's as simple as having each member cook a different dish for dinner or having all the kids cook for the parents.

FAMILY FUTURE

Wherever you are with your family, remember that things won't always be this way! Time passes, and relationships change and evolve. Here's what we've noticed about the way things have changed over time.

Amy

My relationship with my family has drastically changed since I was younger. I was a total people pleaser, with zero boundaries back then, and I placed my family above myself in importance. I would always sacrifice my personal needs for the good of the group, as if I could single-handedly keep the group together forever by making sure people were happy all the time and never hurt. I built up a ton of resentment and anger. I didn't realize how never voicing my physical needs and putting myself last hurt me. It made me feel unheard and unseen by the ones I loved most, but I didn't understand at the time that nobody can hear you if you don't speak up. No one made me give up my sense of self; I willingly surrendered it. As I have grown up, I have learned that I can ask for the things I need, that my family really is happy to lift me up and support me when they can,

Instead of taking family time for granted, realize you won't always be able to be together like this.

114

and that I am not responsible for everyone else's health and well-being. That has changed everything for me. I feel more connected and seen now than ever before, and I wouldn't trade my family for anything.

Christina

As I've gotten older, I have gained a new perspective on family and my relationship with my parents. When you're a teenager, you have different focuses than you will when you're an adult. It can be hard to understand things that you haven't been through yet but your parents have, and that can cause your ideas to clash.

I remember at fifteen being annoyed and confused sometimes by my parents' decisions and not always being able to see when they had my best interests at heart. Now looking back, I can see they were doing the best they could with the information they had at the time. I am much more able to give them the benefit of the doubt now—but as a teen, it was hard to see things from their point of view.

I wouldn't trade my family for anything.

If that's you, realize that you won't always understand why they say, do, or want certain things. If you're frustrated and confused, try calmly asking them why. Ask for more information. Hear them out with an open heart. This could lead to more connection, a closer relationship, and maybe even some understanding.

Lisa

I've become so much closer with my mom as I've gotten older, mainly after I moved out. Once I had the freedom to make my own choices, I felt like my own person and could stop resenting her for our past troubles. Now I love hanging out with her and just talking and laughing. It's hard to think back on my younger years and remember all the things I never told her I was going through because I was so terrified of telling people how I felt or what was going on inside my head. But I know the future's ahead of us, and I'm very grateful that I still get to spend time with her and grow closer to her now.

Wherever you are in your family right now, you've got the future ahead of you too. You can take a lot of small steps to help you start working out the negatives and strengthening the positives. And small things done consistently can have a huge impact over time. Who knows? Maybe focusing on some good communication, problem-solving, or family bonding will have a major payoff down the line, when you're able to enjoy strength and support from your family ties.

JOURNAL

- Have you ever felt isolated within your family? How can opening up about your feelings help you be less isolated in your family?
- Think about each individual member of your family. What are their personalities like? If you were to start practicing seeing the best in them and reaching out to them, what would that look like?
- Have any unhelpful communication patterns been the norm in your family? How can you spot each pattern and try a different one?

PRAY

God, thank You for the gift of family. I pray for each member of my family, for their health, safety, and healing. I pray for all of my family relationships and ask You to guide us to be as close and healthy as possible. Please help me enjoy and get to know these people while I can, and show us how to make each other's lives better through acceptance and love.

CHAPTER 6
MONEY

WHEN EACH OF US BECAME teenagers, our parents stopped buying anything extra for us beyond food and clothes. If we wanted to buy something, we babysat, walked dogs, filed documents, did chores, or did pretty much anything we could to get some extra cash. They also purposely bought us smaller, less extravagant gifts for our birthdays and holidays. If we wanted something big, like a digital camera or an iPod, we had to work for months to save up for it.

Although at the time it didn't make sense to us, looking back we all deeply appreciate this practice because it taught us the value of hard work. Both of our parents, while total opposite personalities, are incredibly smart and hardworking. Our mom achieved a lot as an All-American swimmer, then earned her master's degree in music, and then homeschooled all eleven of us. Our dad worked insane hours growing his construction business and mastering his craft in order to provide for all of us. Because of his hard work, we were able to try any sport we wanted and participate in musical theater and many enriching activities growing up that profoundly shaped our character.

Their amazing example of hard work deeply affected us, and we made the important connection between hard work and money. While some of us are more experienced with money than others, we learned a few things from becoming entrepreneurs and business-women at a young age. In this chapter, we'll share some basic tips for growing a healthy relationship with money.

THE EMOTIONS BEHIND MONEY

What profit is there for one to gain the whole world and for-feit his life?

MARK 8:36

Katherine

We rarely talk about the emotional component to money, but it's such an important thing to know about ourselves. We all have a different emotional reaction to money since it plays an essential role in our survival and well-being. Most of our view of money is formed in our homes. If you grew up in a family where your parents were constantly stressed about making ends meet or fighting about money, you might have a very negative association with it, and understandably so. Or if you grew up in a wealthy family that strongly associated self-worth with how much money a person has, you would also have a negative view of money, just in a totally different way.

Money can be like a drug. When you see something you like, a

MONEY

lot of times it feels like you need it NOW; spending is a "high" in itself. I think one of the most important aspects of money is being self-aware about our habits and really examining ourselves as we are going about our day and making purchases. Are we spending just to numb pain? Are we spending because we think we can buy happiness or freedom? Is this purchase something we need, or just something we bought to distract from our problems? How do we figure out our own emotional motivations around money?

When I think of money, I think of plane tickets to visit friends in different states. I think of buying my friends nice birthday gifts that make them smile. I also think part of it—especially because of how media and advertising manipulate women—is about power. I think women commonly get the message that their power lies solely in how they look. This in turn causes us to spend thousands of dollars on skin and hair care products, new out-fits, haircuts and treatments, makeup, perfume, basically anything to look and feel beautiful and valued. When I think of having to wear the same old clothes that maybe aren't as trendy anymore, or not being able to buy a new makeup product I think would look good on me, I feel insecure. That sounds silly to admit, but it's true.

Money can be like a drug. . . . spending is a "high" in itself.

On the flip side, there are some very necessary purchases we have to make that also have an incredibly emotional component to them. I bought my first car four years ago, and that was one of the proudest moments of my life, knowing I had worked hard to save the money. Same thing goes for my first house—purchasing that gave me a huge rush of pride! Our attitude toward money just has to be balanced; as long as we are aware of our emotions, we can make good money decisions.

Lauren

It's true that sometimes we buy things we don't need because we are actually really sad and we wanna feel better. For me, I can go a little crazy at clothing stores and buy a bunch of new clothes, which is exciting and feels good for a little bit, but that kind of excitement doesn't last. Another thing I do is buy a bunch of comfort food and try to feel better that way. Ultimately, however, nothing you buy is going to change how you feel. You have to just deal with what you are going through.

When I was living with my parents as a teenager, I spent *so much money* on food that I didn't need to buy. My parents fed us, but I thought it was more fun to buy myself treats and meals while we were living in Malibu. So, I would go out all the time for ice cream, sushi, or the gourmet grocery store hot bar (which is basically a million dollars for one crumb). I wish I had known how much a mortgage would cost once I moved out and prepared myself for that more by saving up all that money I spent on random snacks! Yes, it's fun to treat yourself once in a while. But especially when you're living at home and not having to pay bills, it will make your life soooo much easier if you'll save that money for when you'll need it in a few years instead of making yourself feel good emotionally right now.

> *Ultimately, nothing you buy is going to change how you feel.*

Dani

It's true: spending money makes you feel good. You get clothes that are trendy to make you "fit in," buy makeup because it makes you "prettier," or go out to dinner with your friends even though you don't necessarily have the money for that. Being aware of this is so important when it comes to being smart with money because sometimes you end up at the store spending half your paycheck on new clothes that you didn't need simply because you don't think twice about it. Every time I feel the urge to spend, I ask myself, "Do I *really* need this?" or, "Am I *actually* going to use this?" And it has kept me from purchasing so many unnecessary things.

> He who loves money will not be satisfied with money, nor he who loves abundance with its income.
> ECCLESIASTES 5:10

Katherine

If you feel like you're constantly thinking about the next thing you want to buy, and you're never satisfied, I would recommend asking yourself if this is a pattern you see carrying on to other aspects of your life. I know you've heard it before, but what they say is true—money CANNOT buy happiness. Yes, you do need money to live. And lack of it is definitely going to cause you anxiety. But it is an absolute and essential truth: even though there are lots of emotions connected to money, you cannot buy happiness! Lasting happiness comes from a relationship with God, having healthy and strong relationships, cultivating gratitude, and learning how to be content with and grateful for what you already have. Seriously! So many of the things that make us truly happy don't cost anything at all.

SWAPS AND UPGRADES

If you're about to spend money on something for emotional reasons, you have to ask yourself, "Am I trying to get something money can't buy?" Substitute those purchases for something that's as good, if not better—and often free!

Katherine

Swap beauty purchases for cultivating your inner beauty. We want to feel beautiful, so we buy makeup and hair products. But true beauty comes from learning to love what's unique about us, showing love to the people in our lives, and cultivating virtue in our character, such as patience, generosity, charity, and compassion. True beauty is someone who is full of light and who other people want to be around because of how radiant that light is. It is so much deeper than mascara and a good haircut!

Christina

Swap these quick fixes for something better:

- comfort food → a relaxing bath
- brand names to fit in → connecting with true friends
- sugar for the sugar rush → going to a park and having fun like you're a kid again
- buying things to post on social media to up your status → getting off social media and reconnecting with real people in your life instead

HOW IMPORTANT IS SAVING?

Something a lot of older adults say is that, looking back, the one piece of advice they would give their younger selves about money is this: *Save. Start young. Do it!* Saving money is a habit that will pay off in a huge way down the line, and developing the habit now will give you an incredible advantage. Here are our best practices.

Save. Start young. Do it!

Christina

I would always hear people preaching to me about saving money, and for a long time, it went in one ear and out the other. Nothing changed my mind or whipped me into shape like these two things did:

1. Having to pay bills.
2. The idea of having more in my bank account this month than I did last month.

Make the goal to have a certain amount more in your bank account each month and to watch the number go up month by month. After the first few months of watching it go up, you'll be excited and empowered to become even more creative about finding ways to make more money and spend less money.

Lisa

How do you save money? Stop spending it. Ha! Seriously though. Don't spend it. Here are some of my tips on saving money:

- There are so many fun things to do that are *free*. Make a list of your favorite memories from the last few years and put a star next to each thing that didn't cost money. Then think if there's a way you could've made the other items on the list free or at least cost less than they did.
- Food is a HUGE money suck. Try splitting meals, cooking at home, having people over to cook with you, and bringing snacks instead of buying them while you're out. All of those things will help so much!
- Another big money suck is CLOTHING. Go through your closet and identify pieces you haven't worn in a while and other things you could wear with them that you haven't tried yet. Mixing it up is a great way to get more bang for your buck. I love shopping way too much, so feeling like I have new options is always a big help in avoiding hitting up the mall.

Lauren

I know that saving money can be really hard. We want to do all these fun things that cost money. The idea of saving can make you feel like you're in a prison, but actually it frees you!

If you have money saved up, you can do the things you want to do, like buy a car, move out, invest in your passions, or buy a nice camera or software or supplies. You can reach bigger goals with that money.

If possible, and especially when you're living at home with minimal to no expenses, save at least half of your income every month. Put it in a savings account, and *do not touch it*. If you're saving up for something expensive, do not save up until you have that exact amount and then spend your entire life's savings on it. Save enough so that you have a good amount of money left after you buy it.

If you are in the habit of spending all your money as soon as you get it, *stop*. If you have a job, you should have at least $1,000 saved at any given time. This might sound like a huge number, but it doesn't have to be that hard. Look for little ways to save. Get creative. You will be so much more in control of your life if you start building a cushion of savings.

⋯⋯⋆ FUN, FREE THINGS TO DO ⋆⋯⋯

- movie night at home
- playing hide-and-seek on your street in the summer
- baking/cooking dinner (with food you already have)
- walking around your neighborhood
- going to a park
- going somewhere with a cool view
- making weird/fun videos
- going to free events in your town
- listening to music
- learning something new on YouTube
- taking a free local class of some sort (check online to see what's available in your area)
- exploring your town on a walk or on a bike
- drawing or taking pictures

- making up a dance with your friends and filming a video
- going on walks with your friends or hanging at each other's houses instead of going to coffee or out to eat
- giving a friend a "makeover": doing her makeup and hair and picking her outfit (or you can do it for each other)
- reorganizing your room so it feels new
- getting a group of friends together for an outdoor game—the more people, the more fun it is! (Use Google to find ideas of games)

Katherine

I am not a naturally thrifty person. I have a huge appetite for life, and I want to experience everything—every road trip, concert, dinner at a fun restaurant, and night out with friends. Being a very social person and being thrifty do not seem to go hand in hand.

But it helps if I focus on the positive aspects of saving money. Where I used to equate saving with being bored and missing out on fun things, now I focus on the good things about saving, such as freedom and being financially secure, which also means being more relaxed and less stressed! There is also the serious side of saving, such as having a "rainy day fund," which basically means having money saved in case of emergency.

Several years back, I had a really stressful situation where I had to pay out of pocket for an expensive oral surgery, and I was not financially prepared for it. My tooth was basically dying in my mouth out of the blue—something you never would expect to happen in your early twenties! I had the down payment saved up, but the second half took me over a year to pay off. I had never been in any debt before, and I felt so deeply ashamed. When I finally finished paying it off, it felt as though a huge weight was off my shoulders.

Since then, I have worked hard to live in a more disciplined way when it comes to saving, and I am happy to say I learned to live on a budget and save up the extra money I never had as a teenager! It's such a comforting feeling knowing that if a surprise expense comes up, I can pay for it without worry.

HOW TO BUDGET

Saving and budgeting go hand in hand. But does the word *budget* make you want to hide under a rock? Do you associate it with *It's time to take back budgeting and call it what it is: planned freedom.* boredom and eating plain oatmeal and canned soup? It's time to take back budgeting and call it what it is: *planned freedom*.

Amy

Money can be a source of great stress or a great tool. It all depends on the habits you make when spending it.

The basic principle of budgeting is as follows: *spend less than you make*.

You make a budget by first figuring out how much you make a month, and then you figure out what you spend your money on. Finally, you figure out how much of that you are willing to spend on the things you want and need.

Let's say you make $500 a month. A budget would look like this:

$500	total
$75	gas
$75	eating out and fun money
$75	shopping
$275	saving

Now you try. Maybe you need to keep track of your spending for a month in a little notebook or on your phone so you know where the money is going. Once you know, divide it up into your categories, and make your budget official. Stick to your budget and save your money. That's how you make good money habits!

You may be asking, *But what if I'm completely broke? Where is all that budgeting money going to come from?* Don't stress. You can look into a few ways you can make money over the summer and through the school year. Having a job can help you feel empowered and productive. It can help you get the skills you will need later in life. Working at different places is also a good way to find what you want to do for a career.

Here are a few examples of places you can work or tasks you can perform to jump-start your income:

- a movie theater
- a restaurant
- a store
- lifeguarding at a pool
- babysitting
- odd jobs
- mowing lawns
- teaching some sort of lessons

Making a starter income and handling that income wisely will put you well on your way toward a good financial future.

Amy

I am not a financial planner or professional finance person, but I've read that you should figure out your expenses in your budget and have at least six months of them saved. This applies more to later in life, when you live on your own. If you have this money saved, you could even move somewhere fun or start a new venture. You will be okay if you suddenly lose your job because you have that money set aside. This will *greatly* reduce your stress as you get older. Saving your money and using it wisely will help you have a more secure and stress-free future!

Dani

I want to talk for a minute about sticking to that budget you just made. You *have* to be strong when your friends want you to spend extra money you don't have. Be honest with your friends, and stay out of situations where you could potentially spend extra money and mess up the budget. So, for example, if your friends always want to go out, don't say you'll go with them and not spend if you are prone to spending. And don't try to hide the fact that you're saving! Be real and just say, "I'm saving for *x*, so if you could help me out by doing more free things, that would be really helpful." If you're saving for something really amazing or important, that's something to be proud of. Saving and budgeting your money isn't lame, stupid, or something to be ashamed of. Your friends should support and help you—and if they don't, maybe they're not true friends.

MONEY TOOLS

Once you've got yourself in a saving and budgeting frame of mind, there are all sorts of tools you can use to keep you on track and get you where you want to go.

CHECKING AND SAVINGS ACCOUNTS

Amy

The first thing you should do when you start making money is open up a savings account. (Ask your parents for help if you are under eighteen.) The first step is to research banks. Once you have found the bank you want to use and that makes the most sense for you, call them up and make an appointment. You can also ask if you can set up an account online. Then they will walk you through all the steps when you open your account with them.

In the beginning when you are starting out with budgeting, it can be helpful to withdraw all the physical money you want to spend that month and only use cash. Leave your card at home. Cards involve a lot of self-discipline so you don't go into debt. Once you have mastered discipline with paper money, you can move on to a card.

A WORD ON CREDIT CARDS

Lisa

My main advice with credit cards is to treat them like a debit card. Don't get in the habit of spending money you don't have! Always keep track of how much you have in your account so you know you have enough to pay off your credit card every month. Also, make sure to set an alarm on your phone each month a few days before your bill is due, and pay it a little early. That's my go-to trick for avoiding late fees.

MONEY APPS

Christina

For technology, I enjoy using the app Mint because it shows me how much I've spent on each category, how much cash I currently have in my accounts, and if I'm overspending in a category when I may not have noticed.

Lisa

I love apps that help you keep track of spending! There are a lot of good options that will analyze your income versus spending and give you regular updates of where your accounts are. If you're not comfortable giving your banking information to a third party, you can always use your Notes app to jot down how much you're spending on food and entertainment each time you make a purchase. I know that might sound tedious to some, but it REALLY helps to know how much you're putting down each month (especially if you're just starting out), and it only takes a few seconds to write things down. If you don't know how much you're spending or what you're spending it on, how can you know what to work on and improve? Knowledge is power, so make sure you know!

QUESTIONS TO ASK YOURSELF

Katherine

Last year I got really into a concept called *minimalism.* I read books on it, watched documentaries and YouTube videos on it, and read articles as well. It's definitely a trendy word right now. I think a lot of people assume it means to literally get rid of everything you own down to the bare necessities. But I took a less extreme approach: I started to ask myself questions and simplify my life.

I went through all my shoes, clothes, books (this one was the hardest 'cause I *love* my book collection), and other belongings and asked myself if each item really was useful or brought value to my life. I was surprised to realize I had a lot of things I held on to and I wasn't even really sure why. Getting rid of them freed up space in my house, and my environment felt lighter and more open.

It all comes back to being self-aware and asking yourself, "Do I really need this? Or even want it?"

This especially affected the way I now buy things. It's easier to realize I'm being careless and decide not to purchase something. I think it all comes back to being self-aware and asking yourself, "Do I *really* need this? Or even want it?" and with clothing especially, saying, "Do I *love* this? Or just kind of like it?" Find your own money philosophy and ask yourself questions that point you back to it. If you figure out what you're going to do ahead of time to remind yourself of your goals, there's less struggle in the moment.

Lauren

I love fashion, and I love buying new clothes. But to make sure I don't overspend, I have a trick: I don't look at the tag before I try it on, and then once I have it on, I tell myself how much it's worth. Like, *Okay, this shirt is cute, but I would only pay ten bucks for it.* Then, if you check the tag and it's fifteen dollars, you don't buy it!

Also, if you have something you are saving for, use that as a tool to stop yourself overspending. Just remind yourself of how good you will feel once you have saved up the money for that car or that new phone or that concert or that trip! Ask yourself, *How much more important is my goal?*

YOUR MONEY FUTURE

If you've been in church much, you may have heard the term *stewardship*. That's the idea that we are simply guardians of the money and resources God has given us, and we get to steward or manage them well. That affects the way we save, spend, and give. It also affects the way we look at our future. How can we be smart about what's to come?

Amy

Right now I am saving up for my future. I am saving so I can invest money easily and have a good safety net. But I haven't really thought about where faith and money intersect until recently. We are cared for and loved by God, who wants to help us and provide for us. He gives us so much, and it is our responsibility to help others with what He has given. I have recently started giving a tithe (10 percent of one's income given to a church or to God's work in the world). I think that is a great way to say thank You to God and that you trust in Him to provide for you. You are literally giving of what He has given you so that others may be helped by His abundance!

> Each must do as already determined, without sadness or compulsion, for God loves a cheerful giver.
>
> 2 CORINTHIANS 9:7

Christina

When I got engaged, and even before then, I knew Nick and I were saving for our wedding, to buy a house, and to furnish our house. There is *always* something to save for in your future. Your first or next car, first or next house or apartment, a dream you want to be able to fund, school, everything! We don't often look ahead a year or two when it comes to finances, and then we are shocked when we don't have the money we wish we had to make these big, necessary purchases. But this can be avoided by looking ahead at the next ten years and asking, "What kinds of things will be coming up that I need to make goals for?"

My current savings goals revolve around the next several years, not the next several weeks or even months. I want to be a good steward of my money. To me, this means tithing, avoiding becoming greedy and worshiping material things and money, and not giving in to the temptation to use money to impress others. When I make purchases, I normally consider whether I really *need* what I'm buying, what my *intention* is in buying it, and whether this is the *wisest* use of my money. Sometimes I mess up. Sometimes I get overly excited and don't think things through. But I always come back to my financial goals and values and get myself right back on track as soon as I can.

What kinds of things will be coming up that I need to make goals for?

When I want to buy something I'm not sure about, I make myself wait. I add it to my cart online but tell myself I can't buy it until next month, or I just wait a week or two. Most of the time I don't even end up buying whatever it was. Impulse purchases will get you! That's why I need that strategy. It works for me.

Amy

When I was younger, I used saving money as an outlet for my control issues. I felt like the more money I saved, the more in control I was, and spending money would make me feel out of control. I was also too scared to take full responsibility for my finances by making a budget. It is okay to spend money. It doesn't mean you are out of control, and fearfully saving money with no real goal won't make you safe. Don't be scared to take control of your financial life. Money can cause a lot of stress, but it doesn't have to. Just budget smartly and trust that God will provide for you.

Christina

When I was a teenager, I thought that when I could afford to buy most things I wanted, this would make me super happy and be so exciting. I didn't realize that the "happiness" gained from buying things doesn't last very long. It's really nowhere near as exciting as I thought it would be. I'd tell my younger self not to worry so much about money but also not to idolize it. Worry doesn't help in making plans and taking action, and idolizing money only takes you down a misleading path. The money mind-set that has made me the most peaceful is making plans for the future, being knowledgeable about my money and where it's going, knowing my goals, and ultimately focusing on influencing myself and others positively with not only my money but also my time.

> Those who trust in their riches will fall
> But like green leaves the just will flourish
> PROVERBS 11:28

JOURNAL

- Think about the emotions you have around money. The last time you made an emotional purchase, what were you *really* trying to buy?
- If you don't have a budget, use a page of your journal to sketch out your expenses and income. Take a few days to keep track of a typical week, and then make it firm. Does anything surprise you about your budget?
- What are your hopes for your money future? How can what you're doing today build habits to get there?

PRAY

God, help me cultivate a healthy attitude toward money. Show me how to seek wisdom and knowledge, and guard my heart from greed and impulsive decisions. I want to use my resources the absolute best way I can!

CHAPTER 7
YOUR
FUTURE

WHAT COULD YOUR FUTURE LIFE hold? What will your career be? What kind of person will you turn out to be years from now? We've all spent lots of time wondering what the future would bring us. We've dreamed dreams and felt anxiety, made plans, and struggled with decisions. And we know you're probably doing the same. We want to encourage you to make big goals and not be afraid to go after what you really want in life! Lots of people will tell you what you *should* do, but only you can decide what you *will* do.

Growing up in our family and choosing music as a career, we never fit into a box. In our small town, a lot of people criticized us and tried to discourage us from being a band and hoping to make a career out of it. In their minds, they were probably trying to protect us from the harsh realities of rejection and the "real world." I mean, can you really blame them? We probably seemed crazy when we first started our band, just a band of teenagers and preteens in a small town. Why would anyone have faith that one day we would achieve great things?

Twelve years later, we've released four albums of songs we wrote, toured all over the world, and, greatest of all, been given the chance to share our music and message with girls like you. We've experienced incredible things—things we never dreamed possible.

Lots of people will tell you what you should do, but only you can decide what you will do.

But our greatest accomplishment is truly that we never gave up, even after countless mistakes, lots of rejection, and tons of failures. We had to learn those lessons, just like we continue to learn lessons, fail, and make mistakes.

We want to encourage you not to be afraid of failure. To think outside the box for your future, even if that means stepping outside of "normal" to do something incredibly unusual. With some thought and reflection, you can find your passions and use them to choose to do something with your life that you truly love. It will not be easy, but it will be worth it.

MIND-SET

Nothing affects our decisions in life more that our mind-set—or the direction of our thinking. The most empowering moment is when you realize you can choose that direction. You're in control. Here are our thoughts on cultivating the kind of mind-set that will take you where you want to go in your future.

Do not conform yourselves to this age but be transformed by the renewal of your mind, that you may discern what is the will of God, what is good and pleasing and perfect.

ROMANS 12:2

Amy

The biggest challenge we face in our lives is learning to control our thoughts. The way we think about ourselves affects how we interact with the world. When we see ourselves as worthy of love, we act with love and compassion. When we learn to forgive ourselves, we can forgive others more freely. When we are compassionate with ourselves, we are more compassionate with others. We can make every situation better or worse, depending on how we think about it.

When you wake up, be thankful for your new start!

When something happens and we automatically go to the negative aspect of the situation, that can take us down a long, dark, and winding path that can derail our future. If someone discourages us, we can either go, "Ugh! How could this happen to me? I don't deserve this. How could they say that to me?" or we can take the more positive approach of "This is only a small setback; I can try again." Every morning you can wake up and be grateful that you're alive, or you can wake up tired and negative, dreading the day ahead. When you wake up, be thankful for your new start! Life, and your future, is all about how you think about it.

Challenge your mind-set. If you come up against a setback

on your way to reaching your dreams, instead of thinking, *What is wrong with me?* think, *What is wrong with my thinking?* You can always change the way you think!

Christina

Few things in life should be taken more seriously than cultivating a healthy, positive mind-set. It all starts with how you talk to yourself. Whether you're aware or not, there's a conversation going on in your head throughout the entire day, every day.

Sometimes it's conscious, but other times it's more of a subconscious voice. Sometimes it's not even you talking, but you're replaying quotes from the past—things other people have said. Maybe you even hear a meaner, more critical voice. Whatever it may be, it's up to you to control that constant conversation.

The tricky part about changing the conversation from one that drags you down to one that empowers you is that it's not enough to simply "stop the negative thinking." Instead, every negative thought *must* be replaced by a positive one if a positive change is to take place. This is all about awareness and effort. Become aware of what you are thinking throughout the day, and make the effort to consciously give yourself pep talks and say positive things. Replace all those negatives with positives; this will change your life drastically.

⋯⋯✦ REPLACING NEGATIVE ✦⋯⋯ THOUGHTS

If you're constantly battling the same negative thoughts, you can plan ahead with the positive thoughts you want to replace them with. Some people use encouraging scriptures for this, and some use positive affirmations that reflect the way things *really* are instead of allowing their minds to go down that negative path. Here are a few examples:

Negative	Positive
I can't do anything right.	I'm allowed to make mistakes. I learn from them and get better every day.
I'm too scared.	I am courageous and brave.
I should just give up.	Tomorrow is always a fresh start. I will keep going.
I'm not good enough.	I'm getting better every day in every way!
I'm annoying.	I love and embrace who I am.
I have nothing to offer this world.	I have so much to offer this world. I will find and share my specific gifts with people!
I hate my body.	I am learning to love my body.
I'm stupid.	I am learning more and getting smarter each day.
I have no friends.	I am making friends. I am friendly, and people like me!
I can't do this.	I will keep trying until I can do this.

The world, unfortunately, is full of negative messages. We get these from the media, people who don't like us, people we work with, and sometimes even our friends and family members. Sometimes they mean to hurt us, and sometimes they don't. That's why we need to protect our mind-set. It's so important to talk back to the negative voices in your head and develop an automatic, habitual way of talking ourselves back up when we've been brought down. Putting in the daily effort to make this way of thinking a strong habit will be some of the best time you've ever spent; I know it has been for me!

Dani

When you think about your future life, you should ask yourself one simple question: What really matters?

Find what you love, and do exactly that—not just because you should do what you want in life but because you're going to be the best at doing things you truly enjoy. People find it so stressful choosing what college they're going to, picking a person to date, deciding on a career, or just making decisions in general. However, it's really not that stressful if you simply *do things you actually like*. Don't be friends with people you don't like. Don't go to a college that you don't like just because your parents like it. Don't date someone because you feel like you should be in a relationship. You are in control of your own life. Let me say that again: *you are in control of your own life*. Breathe, sit, stand, cry, scream, eat, drink, *live* that sentence. Even though it might not seem like it sometimes, *you are in control* of the things that matter. You literally do not have to do anything with your future that you don't want to do, and you especially don't have to listen to other people trying to make decisions for you. Stand your ground. Find what you love, and live a life you actually like. You deserve to live a happy life, and you definitely don't deserve to look back on an average life that you weren't even in control of.

Your path in life is going to be bumpy, confusing, and at times stressful, but it's all heading toward your destiny. I believe that God has a special place where I'm supposed to end up and that He has a plan for my life. You have to trust yourself, make your own decisions, and make them as smart as you can, but remember that it's okay to mess up. You don't have to have everything figured out. Just take it one step at a time, and live the life you love—because you have a choice. You can live your unique life, or you can live someone else's.

Even though it might not seem like it sometimes, you are in control of the things that matter.

> "I know the plans that I have for you," declares the LORD, "plans for welfare and not for calamity to give you a future and a hope."
>
> JEREMIAH 29:11

Lisa

Nobody likes failure, but you *can* develop a mind-set that will turn your failures into strength for the future. Every major success story is full of failures leading up to it. The best lessons we learn in life are from our failures.

Things go wrong before they go right. Get that into your mind. Anyone who ridicules you for falling down probably hasn't stood up much in their life. You're gonna get noticed if you try, and some people

Anyone who ridicules you for falling down probably hasn't stood up much in their life.

are uncomfortable with that because it makes them think about how little effort they put in and about all their regrets. It hurts them to face that. They'll try to bring you down and stop you so they can feel comfortable again. They want you to fail and be invisible so they can feel comfortable in their own invisible life of failure! *Do not be a cushion on their couch of mediocrity!* (Lol. Okay, Lisa, chill.)

Anyway, don't shape your life around other people's feelings like that. It's not only unhealthy but destructive. You *must* put up boundaries. This is *you*. This is where you begin and you end. This is what *you* want to do. This is what *you* need. This is how *you* are going to get it.

PASSION

Do you know what your passions are? What makes you excited about life? What can you do for hours on end and not notice any time has passed at all? If you're thinking about a certain thing, great—you can develop it and let it inform your career decisions in the future, making it more likely that you will be happy and fulfilled in your job. If you can't think of anything you are passionate about, don't worry. Now is the time in your life when you might just be figuring that out. Let's take a moment and reflect on what our passions are and where they come from.

Katherine

Passions are those things we do without much effort—the things that come easily and that we really enjoy. For me, those passions are writing poetry, baking, music, and other random things, like public speaking and fund-raising for a cause I believe in. The options are truly endless. I encourage you to spend at least a little time every day doing something positive that makes you feel alive. Don't push it aside 'cause you're too busy, or you may find that your life begins to feel gray and meaningless.

Christina

It seems like knowing what you are passionate about would be very easy. For some people, it is. But most of us have at least some interests and passions buried deep down within our hearts, waiting to be discovered. They get buried there for many reasons. Maybe we thought they were unacceptable and denied them, or someone told us we shouldn't, so we believed them. Maybe we weren't very good at something, so we told ourselves we didn't like it—or maybe we just haven't discovered what we like yet.

I say, let's jump in and figure it out.

Discovering, uncovering, and living out our passions to the fullest is one of the greatest joys in life. To reach the end of the journey here on earth and realize you didn't pursue what you're passionate about would be a tragedy. When you find things that make you happy and give you a great gut feeling—and that bring good into this world—hold on to them tightly and never give up on them.

When you find things that make your heart happy and give you a great gut feeling—and that bring good into this world—hold on to them tightly and never give up on them.

On top of trying new things, you can also take tests to find out more about yourself. I recommend taking the StrengthsFinder test, which you can find in a print book form or online. The Myers–Briggs test offers career suggestions for each personality that are interesting, and our mom always suggested the book *What Color Is Your Parachute?* by Richard N. Bolles.

Dani

The only way to know what you like is to try stuff. You can watch TV shows or documentaries about people doing certain jobs, do research on what being a nun in a convent is like, or see how much money lawyers make. It can be so fun to discover the different possibilities in life; you just have to put in a little time.

The life you choose doesn't have to be just one thing. . . . And that is okay.

Something I want to stress is that the life you choose doesn't have to be just one thing. You could go to college for teaching and think that you're going to be a teacher for the rest of your life, but then after ten years of doing it, you decide you want to move to Thailand and be a fisherman. And that is okay. If you want to run away and catch fish, go catch fish! There isn't some set-in-stone handbook on what your various life steps have to be. You are a human who is constantly changing, not a robot who was built to complete one task over and over again.

Just start with how you feel now. Read up on different careers and life paths, and see what feels right. Try stuff out, fail a couple times, learn some lessons, and find yourself.

Amy

Life happens. You have two choices: you can let it happen to you, or you can plan and take your future by the hand. Things come at you fast. All of a sudden you're a teenager and forced to decide on what you are gonna do for the rest of your life. People tell you, "You're too young to think about that," then, in the blink of an eye, they're like, "Why haven't you been planning your entire future?!" It can be very stressful.

We are born into this world having a place somewhere. We all have amazing gifts and talents—we just have to figure out how to use them the best we can. Don't think that if you love something and it isn't glamorous, you should give it up. If you have a passion for working with children, there are so many ways to do that. If numbers are your thing, there are countless things you can do with them. When you find what you think you'd like to do, you should talk to people who work in that field and try out internships. That's one way to figure out all the different career options and what you actually connect with. There are *so* many jobs out there. The possibilities are infinite!

Lisa

"Believe in yourself so much it makes other people believe in you." This is one of my favorite sayings and has driven me to jump into some amazing projects that I was previously unsure if I could handle. Now that I'm releasing my own music in addition to the music I've always worked on with my sisters, I am learning just how much work it takes to make things happen

Believe in yourself so much it makes other people believe in you.

Don't be scared to spread your wings! on your own. I have so many stories and visions I want to share with the world, and sometimes I question if I can really make it all happen, but I know that nobody else is going to do it for me. I have to just jump in and try. Don't be scared to spread your wings! If small-minded people are scared by your big dreams, stop sharing them around that crowd, but keep believing in them. Somebody is gonna do the thing you're dreaming about. Somebody is going to pull it off. Someone is gonna see it all through. Why shouldn't it be you?

SUPPORT

Getting to know yourself is one of the best ways to start preparing for your future. But you're also going to need help. You can't do it alone. You're going to need a support system. While every person's path is unique, the world is full of people with valuable experience and wisdom that you can use. Seek them out, ask them questions, read, explore, and keep an open mind. You just might find some advice or direction that changes your life.

Lisa

I can't tell you how much validation from experienced musicians I look up to has stuck with me. I've had people tell me I know what I'm doing since I was seventeen years old, and that the countless hours of practice I put in throughout my teenage years has paid off. That's incredibly encouraging, and it's kept me going in my down times. Some of the best advice I've ever gotten was from a mentor of mine who told me to find the people who understand me and stick with them, and never to mold myself for the masses. I always remember that, and it helps me make decisions to ask myself, *Am I doing this because I believe in it or because I think other people will?*

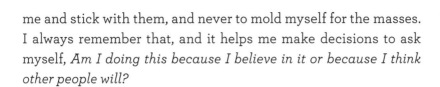

Katherine

My parents are two of the people I trust the most in the world when it comes to career and life advice. They are both so hard-working and smart, yet they also are both big dreamers who aren't afraid to think outside the box and take risks. I regularly share what I want to do in my life with both of them, knowing that they will not only encourage and inspire me but give me helpful advice too.

A few months ago, I was sharing with my mom how my biggest dream is to be a successful author, but I was scared to finish my first book that I'm writing by myself because . . . *what if?* What if I finish it and no one likes it? What if I fail? What if I don't become a *New York Times* best seller? She said to me, "You're putting way too much pressure on yourself. Look, if you get to be in your fifties or sixties and you haven't done this, think of all the regrets you'll have. Just finish the book. Then, at the very least, you can print out *one* copy, put it on your coffee table, and know that you did it. You finished it."

She inspired me so much that I made more progress in a few months than I did in years. I know not all parents are so encouraging, and I'm really grateful that my mom and dad are the way they are!

Reach out to adults and mentors you trust, and share your dreams and fears about the future. With the help of your community, you can get closer to your dreams.

CHANGE IS GOOD

Everything changes. And that's perfectly okay! Part of life is setting a course with intention, but then not being afraid to go down a new side road as it presents itself. Even if you never know where you'll end up, if you keep trying and aiming for a purposeful life, you will end up somewhere great.

Katherine

Growing up, I had so many different ideas of jobs I wanted to do. The first job I ever wanted as a kid was to "make books." I would glue scraps of fabric to construction paper for the cover, then hole punch a bunch of pages together to make a little book. Then I would write stories or poems inside and illustrate it with pictures. I remember my first book was called *Lilly's Adventure to the Wondrous Land*.

Then, when I was around nine or ten, I became fascinated with archaeology after reading some books on it. I was convinced I would spend my time digging for dinosaur bones and ancient artifacts when I grew up. When I got into my early teens, I became obsessed with fashion. I told all my friends I would be a fashion designer. My mom got me a bunch of books on fashion design, and I started studying them and drawing sketches to prepare for my career.

Next, I became interested in researching diseases. Over the course of a year, I read an entire book on diseases that was more than a thousand pages long! At that point I wanted to be a researcher at the Centers for Disease Control and Prevention.

You may be surprised reading this, knowing my full-time job now is as a member of this band with my sisters! The point is, you may end up doing something totally different than you thought you would as a kid. And I'm only twenty-seven now, so

You may end up doing something totally different than you thought you would as a kid.

I definitely plan on doing a lot of different things throughout my life! Who knows? Maybe I'll dabble in a lot of my previous interests in the years to come. I hope to have many years ahead of me, and I want to live a colorful, interesting life!

Christina

When I am facing changes or career decisions, I always ask God for guidance. I ask Him to point me in the direction He would have me go and to give me strength, courage, and wisdom along the way. That way I don't have to depend on my own limited wisdom and vision. I can trust in Him and His plan. I have always gotten these "gut feelings" and feelings of peace leading me in the direction I needed to go. I remember when I was a teenager, around fifteen or sixteen, I would talk all the time about how I was going to pursue music. So many people around me doubted me and shot me down. Not only people my age, but plenty of parents. They thought I had no plans and that it was too far-fetched of a dream, but I was studying, working, praying, and trusting during that time. I had this crazy idea that I had to have a career that would greatly impact others. I knew I badly wanted to be a role model for young girls because I had almost no one to look up to at the time.

While at first I may have gotten a bit too excited about money, fame, and power when I thought of a music career, that drastically changed over time. Really, being a role model was the foundation of my future vision. I wanted to make a positive impact. I wanted to lead. And that desire has led me to some surprising places.

I believe that when you base your goals and dreams on a good intention and a positive plan, you give yourself your best shot at making something happen. You have to know that people will try to tear you down, that not everyone will support you, and that you'll have failure after failure to deal with. This is so normal. I wish we didn't demonize failure as some embarrassing thing to be avoided in our culture. I wish that every young person knew that failure is how we learn. It's how we grow. It's a completely necessary step in the direction of success if we take lessons from it.

When you base your goals and dreams on a good intention and a positive plan, you give yourself your best shot at making something happen.

Amy

I used to be terrified when I would think about my future. I didn't know how to plan for it. I don't like changes when I don't know how they will turn out. It's like being in limbo between knowing that things will probably be fine, but they could still fall apart on me. But I was only thinking of my future in terms of *me*. I was totally ignoring God's plan for me. It's like trying to chart a course when you don't have a map, and frankly don't even know where you are going. It has taken me a long time to actually understand what people mean when they talk about following God's plan and discernment. I was only relying on myself to set myself up for my future. God has an incredible plan for me, and I wasn't even trying to find out what it was. Alone we cannot do anything, but with God all things are possible. That has become my mantra. I may still not know exactly where my future will lead, but I do know that God will be there fighting for me and loving me. If the future is in God's strong and loving hands, then it will be good in the long run, no matter what suffering we experience.

Lisa

I'm so grateful for the changes in my life over the past few years, and I'm excited to see them keep coming. I used to want to be the most famous person in the world when I was a kid. My desire to be seen and valued drove me to *think* that my dream was to be seen and valued by the whole world. Now I know that is an impossible and dangerous dream to have. These days I'm more driven by my desire to inspire and help the people who follow me, express myself creatively, and support myself and live comfortably. I know that people are always going to outdo me in some way, and I have gladly accepted that. I know that some people are very rich, extremely successful, and loved by many, yet they still are deeply unhappy with their lives because what they're longing for can't be provided by strangers or large sums of money. I know that having people think you're doing better than they are financially won't bring you any meaning or peace in the middle of the night when you're all alone and the rest of the world is asleep. I have stopped fighting for the approval and admiration of the rest of society and am focused on living

> *Having people think you're doing better than they are financially won't bring you any meaning or peace in the middle of the night.*

my truth for the good of myself and others, whatever that means to me each year. If I'm more developed emotionally or spiritually than I was the year before, I'm happy with my life. And if I'm not, all I'm focused on is how I can pull that off in the year ahead of me. I'm ready for more and better changes!

Dani

Since I was nine, our band has been my whole life. That made me different from my friends. Everyone around me was in school, and I was going to meetings in LA with record labels. Because of this, I felt *so* different. I wanted to fit in so badly. So when I was around fifteen, I decided to pretend my band didn't exist and immerse myself in the "real world" of teenagers who were "normal." For a while it felt so good to fit in and forget about responsibility, but as I got older and closer to my twenties, I looked at my life and realized it wasn't what I wanted. I had prioritized fun, friends, and fitting in so much that I barely had morals, goals, or thoughts of the future at all. When I turned eighteen, for the first time in pretty much my entire life, I thought ten years down the line. Where did I want to be? Who did I want to be? How did I want to feel? And what actions did I need to take now to have the life I wanted?

Where do you want to be? Who do you want to be? How do you want to feel? What actions do you need to take now to have the life you want?

For the first time I acknowledged that *everything I'm doing right now, regardless of how young I am, is going to affect me in some way.*

If I pretend the future doesn't exist, it won't make my life better. In fact, it'll just make it worse.

Focusing on saving; growing real, deep relationships; and setting goals has made me feel so secure and happy. More secure and happy than I *ever* felt running around with my high school friends and "having fun." Yes, it's important to be young and have good times, but I've learned that when that became my priority, my life lost meaning and depth because I wasn't living for anything at all. I'm not saying to live in the future, but always remember that a lot of things may seem boring or unnecessary because you're young, but things will change. Thinking about your future is *always* a good idea.

Thinking about your future is always a good idea.

JOURNAL

- Make a list of your passions. Now think about your dreams for the future. How do your passions and dreams for the future intersect?
- Have you ever let failure be "the end" of something in your life? Think about how you've felt about some recent failures. How could they be an opportunity to learn and get better?
- What is your biggest challenge to staying positive? How can you fight back?

PRAY

God, I trust that You have a great plan for my future. Lead me to make wise choices and follow Your lead as I discover the things You made me to do and take joy in. My future is in Your hands!

CHAPTER 8
LETTERS TO OUR YOUNGER SELVES

W E'VE TALKED ABOUT SO MANY things in this book that we wished we'd known when we were younger. They're the kinds of things we tell girls who reach out to us, asking for advice, and that we tell ourselves when we need some perspective. So we wrote some letters to our younger selves with all the things we wish we knew at that age. Maybe you'll recognize yourself in these girls. Maybe you'll feel less alone. Maybe you'll start getting excited about your future and everything it holds. Wherever you are in life, we hope you'll see some hope in here for you!

Christina

Dear fifteen-year-old me,

You're in a strange spot. You don't feel like you fit in at all with people your age. You have a very passionate heart full of dreams, but part of you wonders if they are just dreams because they seem so outrageous. You feel invisible to guys, and you wonder if you will stay invisible forever. You're a fairly confident person in some areas, like leadership, and you always have been. But there are several other areas where you're doubting yourself like crazy, and you just don't know how to speak up or how to feel like you actually belong in the room.

I am here to tell you that you don't have to worry about ANY of this. You are developing strong convictions right now that are not the norm at all, but trust me, it is because of those convictions that you will end up in a place you are very, very proud of ten years later.

You will not look back and regret any of those decisions. I know you feel kind of crazy sometimes, but you're about to be completely shocked by what happens with these dreams you're "crazy enough" to believe in. Just please promise me you'll do everything you possibly can to hold on to that idealistic and hopeful attitude you have . . . It's much, much, much rarer at twenty-five than it is at fifteen.

You're going to blossom with so much confidence you won't even believe it. Sure, you'll never be bulletproof, because you're a human, not a robot, but you're going to develop a very strong sense of self, and you're going to become such a strong leader. You don't need to worry about all those things you're worrying about right now. Honestly, you should just start holding your head high and putting yourself out there *right now*.

If there's one thing I've seen over time, it's that everyone feels like they have no idea if they're doing anything right—some people are just better at bluffing than others. And when it comes to guys, please stop worrying. Stop trying to contort yourself into this mold of what you think they want you to be. Instead, I'd suggest you hold your head high (yes, I'll say it again). Just be *you* and, you know, maybe possibly focus on a few things other than guys for a large part of your day. If you cut that time in half, you could really get a lot of other good things done. Please rest assured, though, you're about to be hit with an avalanche of male attention when you *embrace yourself*, and the one thing I hope you'll do is be much, much, much more picky. If a guy is treating you like you're nothing more than a second thought to him, please cut him off. You will never regret that, but you *will* look back and wish you'd stood up for yourself more.

The last thing I want to say to you is to value yourself more and have faith that things will work out. I know this is hard and you feel so lost and confused, like you're just spinning around aimlessly in this crazy world, but trust me: things are going to be amazing. Crazy things will happen in your life that you just won't even believe. You really don't need to worry *at all*. All you need to do is have strong faith in God and yourself, bravely put yourself out there, and fight for the things you believe in (because sometimes it will be a fight).

Never, ever, ever try to change who you genuinely are to be like someone else. You have these unique qualities for a *reason*. Please start to develop and embrace them now. You won't regret it. You're in for a crazy ride, so buckle up, lady. Oh, and stop thinking you need to be "quiet" as you embrace your personality more. You will never be quiet—so stop trying!

Love,

Christina

Katherine

Dear little Kath,

Thinking of you at thirteen, fourteen, and fifteen, I feel so sad. I see a girl who is deeply insecure and afraid. I see a girl who is desperately trying to get attention from guys and approval from girls, and who fears that something is very wrong with her, and that's why it seems her friends are hypercritical of her and "no boys" are interested in her. For some reason, your world will start revolving around the opinions of others, and you will begin to base a fragile and flimsy sense of self-worth on how your friends and the people around you—especially boys—react to you that day.

It will always be fluctuating up and down, and you will constantly feel on edge, confused, and numb—so full of fear and anxiety that you become out of touch with your emotions and who you truly are. You will start to feel desolate and lost, like you are floating and not really alive.

At around age fourteen, you will have a very negative breakthrough moment—you will decide to become the ultimate people pleaser, and you will also completely close yourself off to boys and not even try to talk to them *ever*, out of fear of rejection.

When I think of you at ages sixteen and seventeen, I feel this huge rush of being proud of you and excited for you. Somehow you managed to kick being obsessive about hating how you looked and thinking you were ugly and unlovable. Somehow you managed to walk away from unhealthy, toxic friends who kept you enmeshed in gossip, criticism, manipulation, and controlling behavior for years.

You will begin to find yourself and love that person. Something tightly wound in you will begin to unravel as you slowly fall a little bit in love with the tall, quirky girl in the mirror. It will look like playing bass at night on the front door step and walking down to the library to stuff your backpack with books to read. You will become highly opinionated about the things you care about and develop a sense of compassion and a thirst for healing and love in the world.

God will be the biggest part of your journey as you encounter Him through prayers that make you shiver and weep with joy and pleasure. You will find in your relationship with Him an unshakable foundation and a safe resting place that nothing on earth compares to.

At age seventeen, God will open up your heart again to a very precious gift He gave you as a kid—your love of writing. Your first major heartbreak and many family problems will bring you back to pen and paper. Before you know it, you will be up late almost every night, pouring out years of bottled emotions and tangled thoughts onto stacks of paper you will hide under your bed in a big, pink box.

I want to tell you—please stop worrying about everything all the time. It's all going to work out. Your twenties are going to be AMAZING. God is going to send you some of the most loyal, true friends, and spending time with them will make you almost cry with gratitude. If you had never gone through all those middle and high school friend problems, you would never appreciate what is coming next. As for boys, the *moment* you stop worrying and obsessing and freaking out and just *relax* and, most important, start loving yourself a teeny bit, it's going to open you up to a flood of boys who will come into your life wanting to date you.

The ironic thing is, you won't receive any validation from them until after you've already started validating yourself.

Kath, enjoy this time. Being a teenager is hard and scary, but it's also magical and exciting. You're going to experience romance that will take your breath away—all after deciding to save your first kiss for your wedding day. People will tell you that you are crazy and that it won't work, but don't worry—it will. Things are going to be hard, and there will be a lot of disappointment in the romance department, but there will also be many moments that feel like you are in a movie, and you will say in your head many times over, *WHAT IS MY LIFE!!!* (In a good way!)

You are beautiful and precious, little teenage Kath! You are goofy and quirky and silly, and you make people laugh a lot. You are super sensitive, and one day you will learn to embrace it and see it as a superpower rather than a burden. You are so fun and caring, and people fall in love with the person you are. You don't have to keep trying to be everything to everyone. Just be authentic, and you will be so much happier.

I love you *so* much! You can do this. Don't give up hope—just start writing, and turn your life over to God.

Love,
Your Twenty-Seven-Year-Old Self

Dear Lisa,

You're older now. It's the future, and you're twenty-six. Well, *we* are twenty-six. We made it! FYI, you're doing really well.

You're totally chill with your body—no more hate crimes forcing yourself to run in the rain as a punishment for eating an extra bowl of cereal. You finally dated someone! Two someones, in fact! And they were both wrong for you, but they had good personalities that you enjoyed, and you learned a lot from both experiences. It was totally worth it. So you can also stop stressing about dying alone, cuz you're definitely gonna meet people pretty soon.

Chill out, girlfriend! And lighten up! Stop being so hard on yourself. That's a recurring piece of advice you're gonna receive throughout your late teens and early twenties, and it's gonna make you tear up cuz it hits you the hardest out of all the things people tell you. You really are waaaaay too critical, but luckily, when you're seventeen, you'll discover a way to use that power for good.

You'll learn you're so critical because you're able to see every detail in people, places, and things. While you can find something flawed about literally anything, you can *also* find something positive about literally anything because you notice so many details. Definitely not a negative trait!

Anyway, you're a great person. Stop thinking you're bad; it's a bogus belief that's weighing you down. You're good. You're full of light, and you deserve to be happy and accomplish things. Everything is gonna be fine, okay? Also, go to bed earlier. Nothing good happens after midnight. You make a lot of bad choices late at night, and you would benefit a whole lot more from a good night's sleep.

Also, you're moving to Tennessee in 2015! Whoa! Curveball! Your lifelong dream of living in the South is finally coming true! It turns out really well, so don't freak out. It's a big change, but it's worth it. Oh, and spoiler alert: you grow

165

your hair out really long for six years, and it's your pride and joy, and then this guy makes you really mad and you cut it all off, but IT'S REALLY LIT AND EPIC AND A GOOD CHOICE. The long hair is gorgeous, but you get bored with it, and it plays itself out. The short hair is fresh and baller. Anyway, chin up, kid—everything's fine. It's just life; it doesn't have to be perfect. You're gonna do great!

Love,
Lisa

Amy

Dear Amy,

First of all, *you deserve to actually be accepted.* You deserve so much more than you accept from people. You deserve to be happy. You also deserve to believe in yourself. You have so much potential, Amy. You are allowed to like yourself. *Self-love is not bad.* You actually are beautiful and need to stop telling yourself you are not.

Stop hating on your body, kid. It deserves to be treated with respect. Amy, you don't need to be scared of opening up to people. They will love you because of your flaws, not despite them! You are worth so much, honey! I know you feel isolated and depressed, but that doesn't define you! You are allowed to want things. You are allowed to respect yourself. Don't let anyone take your joy or confidence away from you!

Your personality is a gift! Not a liability. Being loud is not a bad thing. Having a lot to say isn't a bad thing. *Be honest with yourself.* Only deal in facts and reality. You deserve to love yourself, and every moment of your life you deserve to breathe in all of the beauty around you. You deserve joy and happiness. Don't let pain bring you down. Don't fear it. It is one of your greatest allies! Pain brings you closer to happiness than anything else. It is in those moments when we feel pain that we realize our equal ability to feel joy. Welcome them joyfully into your life as an opportunity to grow and become stronger.

You have so much to give! Never think otherwise. And when you feel like the best part of the day is sleeping, remember that there's so much more out there. When you feel so isolated that you can't imagine ever feeling connected again, remember that connection is around the corner. You only live in someone's shadow if you put yourself in it! You are the brightest star that shines in your galaxy. Don't let anyone tell you otherwise.

Also, *it doesn't matter what people say or think about you.* Keep caring deeply about everyone and everything that you do, Amy—it's one of your greatest assets and strengths. You have the ability to love, and that's the most important thing. No one can ever take that away from you. Forgive freely, Amy. *Forgive freely.* Learn how to trust people and *God.*

Also, stop letting boys jerk you around! You deserve so much more than what you settle for; remember that. Everything is going to work out the way God intends. You are allowed to love yourself. You are allowed to love your life. Be courageous, and never give up, honey. That's all you can ever ask of yourself! Good luck, kid; you are gonna make it.

Love,

Amy

Lauren

To the fifteen-year-old me:

First and foremost, calm down. Stop worrying about everything. Everything is going exactly the way it's supposed to. Stressing about it is so unnecessary. You're just wasting your time when you could be enjoying things! Second, stop being so scared of everything! People will like you. They really will. You're not weird or dumb or incapable of conversing. You're cool and people like you—so stop being scared to put yourself out there.

Say what you're thinking; say what you're feeling; say whatever the heck you want to say! Do the things you wanna do. Stop spending all your time in your room. Go out and find some friends (it is possible), and go do fun things with them. You are in control of your life, and you can do things if you want to. Stop letting everyone else dictate your decisions, and do what you want to do and what you know is right.

Get close with people. Especially your family. Stop avoiding everyone, and stop being mad. Be nice and loving to people, and you will get niceness and love right back! People aren't all horrible; there are a lot of cool people in the world you will connect with, so don't get discouraged.

If a guy wants to talk to you, he will. If he hasn't talked to you for the last six months, he doesn't want to talk to you anymore, and that's not gonna change. Stop holding on to him, and let him go. He's not worth it, he's not that special, and you'll find a lot of guys who treat you way better than he did. Stop chasing boys; let them chase you. Stop basing your self-worth on how guys treat you or how many of them like you/don't like you.

Just because they don't see how cool you are does not mean you're not cool!

Soon you will see: boys do like you. This is just a weird time. But enjoy it because soon you will be very overwhelmed by the number of boys talking to you. Focus on yourself. Treat yourself right. Stop eating so much junk food, and please, please exercise. You deserve to thrive and be happy, so start doing it. Stop trying to please everyone, and start living the life you want to live! Make goals, and stick with them. Learn things, experience things, get out of your cave, and go live!

Love,

Lauren

Dani

A letter to the girl I used to be:

The first thing nobody told you is that it's okay to cry. I know that right now it feels like crying will make you weak, but the simple truth is that it will make you better.

I know it's going to take a long time for you to get to a place where tears are comfortable, but that day when you go to the beach with your older sister and that Blink-182 song comes on that finally makes you cry will be the best day of your life. It may seem like you just lost someone, but the death of the girl who hid from her emotions is the first day of the rest of your life.

Please stop letting that boy treat you badly. You deserve so much more than what you're getting, and he really isn't worth it. Half-hearted smiles and apathetic words are nothing compared to what your future holds. It may feel like he's the only one who wants you 'cause he's the first boy to give you a second look, but if you hold on just a little bit longer, you'll find someone who will do something worthy of the pain you're in now.

You will experience euphoria and desolation, pure joy and nothing but pain. You will meet a boy who will set your soul on fire and burn you till you're just ashes. He will break your heart and make you watch him do it. He will be your first real heartbreak.

While we're talking about boys, don't be so scared. I know you think you'll regret getting hurt, but the only thing you will ever regret is not living enough to even get hurt. Putting yourself out there is the best thing you'll do for yourself. However, thank you for being careful and not getting into a relationship with that one boy, because you knew how bad the hurt from him not wanting you would've multiplied if you'd let him be your first relationship.

Keep your friends close, and forgive your enemies. I promise you, holding on to your anger toward that person is not going to make you feel better. I know you love holding grudges, but you're forming a bad habit that will cost you in a couple years.

Also, your time in this place is limited. I'm sure it feels like you're stuck there forever, but you'll be gone sooner than you think. One day, shortly before your fifteenth birthday, you'll wake up, and you'll be two thousand miles away from your old home, wishing you'd spent more time with the ones you left behind.

Thank you so much for standing up for yourself. I know there are moments when you're scared to, but you do it anyway, and those are my favorite moments. I'm so grateful that you finally learned how to love yourself, because without that love, you'd have so many more bruises caused by the belief that you deserve disrespect.

Confidence is the most powerful tool you'll ever pick up, so don't be scared of the day you do. Your personality is absolutely incredible, and if you don't believe it now, you will soon.

Trust in God more, please. He is always with you, and I wish you knew that. I love you.

Dani

CONCLUSION

WE BELIEVE IN YOU

WE ARE SO HONORED AND thankful we got to connect with you through this book! We believe it's no accident that it is in your hands, and that it found its way there for a reason. Here are a few more things to take with you as you go—but most of all we hope we've given you some tools to believe in *you*.

Katherine

As this book comes to an end, I want you to ask yourself, Who are the "big sisters" in your real life, blood-related or not? I love talking to my mom, sisters, and friends about my life and asking for their advice and insight. I also have several older women mentors I talk to as well. Big sisters are out there, and I am so glad I've found some of my own! My friend Sandy is a couple decades older than me, and she's such a loving and strong woman. She and I talk on the phone regularly, and she always says, "I love you, honey, and I'm so proud of the woman you are becoming." I feel so encouraged every time I hear her say that. Sometimes, depending on how hard life is, I cry when I hear those words.

I highly encourage you to find your "big sisters." It will improve your life so much to hear stories and insights from women who are a little farther along in life and can tell you what they did in situations similar to yours.

Dani

Growing up, I really didn't feel comfortable asking for advice on the things we talked about in this book. I desperately needed a source to go to when I was confused, and this book is everything I would've wanted. I hope that after reading this, you remember that you deserve to take care of yourself, make good decisions, and form your *own* opinions about the world and how you want to live in it.

Don't just take our advice and try to turn yourself into one of us. Be your true, authentic self. We're just here to give you a little bit of help, because the answers are inside of you already. I encourage you to be the person you were born to be, because there is absolutely nobody else on earth who is like you, and that is *never* going to change.

Christina

I take the title of "big sister" *so* seriously. Since I was a kid, I knew the fact that my sisters were following me, copying me, saying what I said, doing what I did, and believing things just because I told them they were true was something I never should take for granted.

As you go out there and live your life, realize that when you lead, people will follow. We are all called to be leaders in one way or another. You may not see yourself as a leader, but you have what it takes to be one in your own way. We all do. Life is messy sometimes, but if you have good intentions, always be honest, apologize when you're wrong, admit when you don't know the answer, and learn from your mistakes. Like every flower on its journey from a tiny little bud to a flower, you will bloom in your own beautiful way.

Lisa

If you only learn one thing from reading this book, I hope it's how to respect yourself and keep your standards high and healthy. For me, respecting myself and learning when to walk away from someone who doesn't respect or value me have been two things I struggle with most in life. Getting over that and learning how to stand up for what is right and what I deserve in life have been so powerful for me. I wouldn't be where I am today if I'd ignored those lessons, so I hope you guys all get a good grip on your self-respect as you head out into the world. Know that your best is enough, you don't owe anyone your love and affection, and it's okay to stick up for yourself when nobody else is. Love you guys.

Amy

I am so grateful that you have read our first book! I hope you have learned some hashtag helpful hints for your life. I hope you have gotten to know us all better and have been inspired to live your very best life! Know that you have the power to change your life and to be the person God has called you to be. I am so grateful I could help you! I wish you the very best! XOXO, Amy

Lauren

I hope you've learned that you don't need to sacrifice your standards or your needs to please other people or in order for people to like you. I hope you've learned that it's okay to be you and to embrace all of the things that make you unique, because no one else can be a better you than YOU!

NOTES

CHAPTER 2: SPIRITUALITY

1. C. S. Lewis, *Mere Christianity*, rev. ed. (New York: HarperSanFrancisco, 2009).

C. S. Lewis, *The Screwtape Letters,* rev. ed (New York: HarperCollins, 2001).

Jacques Philippe, *Time for God* (New York: Scepter, 2008).

Jacques Philippe, *Searching for and Maintaining Peace: A Small Treatise on Peace of Heart* (n.p.: Alba House, 2002).

Anne Lamott, *Help, Thanks, Wow: The Three Essential Prayers* (New York: Riverhead, 2012).

John and Stasi Eldredge, *Captivating: Unveiling the Mystery of a Woman's Soul* (Nashville: Thomas Nelson, 2005).

Viktor E. Frankl, *Man's Search for Meaning* (Boston: Beacon, 2006).

Saint Teresa of Ávila, *Interior Castle,* Dover Thrift Editions (n.p.: Dover, 2007).

Lloyd C. Douglas, *The Robe* (n.p.: Reader's Digest, 1993).

CHAPTER 3: FRIENDSHIP

1. MotivaShian, "Just Do It," published August 31, 2015, www.youtube
.com/watch?v=ZXsQAXx_aoo.
2. Henry Cloud and John Townsend, *Boundaries: When to Say Yes,
How to Say No to Take Control of Your Life*, rev. ed. (Grand Rapids:
Zondervan, 2017).

RESOURCES

1. Gay and Kathlyn Hendricks, *Conscious Loving* (New York: Bantam,
1990).
    John Gray, *What You Feel, You Can Heal* (Heart, 1993).
    James Pennebaker, *Opening Up: The Healing Power of
Expressing Emotions* (New York: Guilford Press, 1997).
    Henry Cloud and John Townsend, *Boundaries: When to Say
Yes, How to Say No to Take Control of Your Life,* rev. ed. (Grand
Rapids: Zondervan, 2017).

RESOURCES

Christina

We hope that as you close this book, you will start reading another! Reading has opened our minds drastically. The more I read, the more I'm curious about human behavior and the motivations behind our actions. Here are some topics I suggest you look into:

- vulnerability and shame (Brené Brown is good for this)
- birth order psychology
- personality types (I have read so many different books with different theories on personality types that it's ridiculous; I find Enneagram and Myers–Briggs to be the most interesting currently)
- marriage and relationships (especially books written by therapists, because you get an inside look at hundreds of couples)

- psychology of family relationships and behaviors
- psychology of stress and taking care of your emotional, mental, and physical health

Whatever topics you choose, keep reading. Look for solutions, insights, and new ideas and resources. I know making it a habit has changed my life for the better!

Katherine

When Christina started reading psychology books, she would share with Lisa and me what she was learning, and we would talk for hours and hours about it.

I started looking into it myself in my late teens. I would go to the bookstore near our college with Christina and Lisa after classes and read psychology books, and some of the things we learned changed our lives. Some of my favorites were:

- *Conscious Loving* by Gay and Kathlyn Hendricks
- *What You Feel, You Can Heal* by John Gray
- *Opening Up: The Healing Power of Expressing Emotions* by James Pennebaker
- *Boundaries* by Henry Cloud and John Townsend[1]

There are so many resources out there as you get to know yourself and believe in yourself. Books like these can help you keep going strong on your journey!

KEEP IN TOUCH

GET IN TOUCH WITH US!

Follow us on Instagram (@cimorelliband)
Twitter (@Cimorelliband)
Snapchat (itscimorelli)
Facebook: facebook.com/cimorelliband
YouTube (www.youtube.com/user/cimorellitheband)
And check out our website for merch, tour dates,
new music, and more! Cimorellimusic.com